"I don't understand you, Jonathan—"

"Nor I you! That man—Montgomery—he obviously has some sort of proprietorial claim on you—"

"He's my manager, if you really want to know!" Tory glared straight back up at Jonathan as he towered over her.

"Really?" he parried.

"Yes—really!"

"And it's obvious in what way he 'manages' you!"

"Why, you—!" Tory stood up, striding furiously around the table, her arm raised, ready to swing.

Jonathan easily caught hold of it. He pushed her arm back down to her side, long fingers moving down to become entwined with her own, bringing her body up close to his in the process.

His face was very close to hers as they glared at each other. "Looking at you now, your eyes flashing, face flushed—albeit with anger—I could easily give in to the temptation to manage you myself!"

CAROLE MORTIMER says, "I was born in England, the youngest of three children—I have two older brothers. I started writing in 1978, and have now written over 100 books for Mills & Boon. I have four sons—Matthew, Joshua, Timothy and Peter—and a bearded collie called Merlyn. I'm married to Peter senior; we're best friends as well as lovers, which is probably the best recipe for a successful relationship. We live on the Isle of Man."

Some of the characters from *The Secret Virgin* featured in an earlier story by Carole Mortimer, *Bound by Contract* (#2130).

Carole Mortimer

THE SECRET VIRGIN

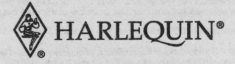

HARLEQUIN®

TORONTO • NEW YORK • LONDON
AMSTERDAM • PARIS • SYDNEY • HAMBURG
STOCKHOLM • ATHENS • TOKYO • MILAN • MADRID
PRAGUE • WARSAW • BUDAPEST • AUCKLAND

My husband,
Peter

ISBN 0-373-12226-8

THE SECRET VIRGIN

First North American Publication 2002.

Copyright © 2001 by Carole Mortimer.

Visit us at www.eHarlequin.com

Printed in U.S.A.

CHAPTER ONE

'JONATHAN MCGUIRE! Would Mr Jonathan McGuire, recently arrived from Heathrow, please come to the information desk?' The message rang out clearly over the airport tannoy system.

Tory stood frowningly beside the desk as the receptionist gave out the message, waiting to see if Jonathan McGuire would respond to it.

She had stood at the door to the baggage reclaim area a few minutes ago, as it opened and closed to allow the people from the Heathrow flight to the Isle of Man to leave once they had collected their cases, a small board held up in front of her with the name of 'Mr J McGuire' clearly written on it. But the last passenger from that flight had gone now, with no sign of Jonathan McGuire.

Maybe he had missed the flight?

Or maybe—

'I'm Jonathan McGuire.'

Tory blinked, and not just at the sound of that huskily attractive American drawl. *This* was Jonathan McGuire?

This man had been one of the first to leave the baggage reclaim area. Tory had noticed him because he was so tall, easily a foot taller than her own five feet two inches in her bare feet, and also because as he'd looked at her, and then through her, with flinty grey eyes, she hadn't been able to help noticing he was one of the most arrogantly attractive men she had ever set eyes on!

His face was ruggedly tanned, and there were those flinty grey eyes, a straight nose, and an unsmiling mouth above a square jaw. The dark grey jacket and white shirt, teamed with the faded blue denims that he wore, emphasised the width of his shoulders, the narrow waist and long, muscular legs. She guessed his age to be somewhere around low-to-mid-thirties. Which was another surprise. Somehow she had had the impression he was Madison's younger, not older, brother.

In fact, he looked nothing like Tory had expected blonde-haired, green-eyed Madison's brother to look!

Which was probably the reason why she had missed him earlier.

But that didn't explain why he hadn't approached her; his name was written very clearly on the board she had held up...

Tory stepped forward before the receptionist could respond. 'I was asked to meet you, Mr McGuire,' she told him lightly, smiling welcomingly.

Those flinty grey eyes were turned on her piercingly, no answering smile on those harshly chiselled features. 'By whom?' he prompted guardedly.

She frowned as his reply, her smile fading; she really hadn't thought, when she'd made the offer to come to the airport this morning, that giving Jonathan McGuire a lift to his sister's home was going to be as difficult as it was turning out to be.

'By your sister,' she murmured, deciding that devastating good-looks didn't go any further than skin deep on this man.

Which was a shame. She had always found Madison one of the easiest people to get along with, had expected her brother to be the same. But he not only didn't look like his sister, he had none of her warm charm, either!

'Madison?' he repeated irritatedly. 'And exactly what is your connection to my sister?' He looked at her critically.

Tory tried to see herself through his eyes: a little over five feet tall, boyishly slender, her almost black hair cut in deliberate ragged layers to fall silkily onto her shoulders, her elfin features bare of make-up; she had dark blue eyes, an upturned freckle-covered nose, a wide mouth and a determined chin. The only thing she had in common with the tall, glamorously beautiful Madison McGuire at the moment was her age; they were both twenty-four!

Her frown deepened as she sensed Jonathan McGuire's criticism of her looks. She liked Madison, was quite happy to do a favour for the other woman, but her brother was turning out to be quite another proposition!

Her second smile wasn't as openly friendly as the first. 'My parents own the farm next to Madison and Gideon's house, keep an eye on things for them while they're away.'

'And?'

Tory was very aware of the avidly listening receptionist. Not that she could blame her. Anyone would think Tory was trying to rob the man instead of offering him a lift!

'Madison telephoned last night and asked me to—'

He scowled. 'Damn it, I asked Gideon not to tell anyone where I was going!'

'Madison is his wife...' Tory pointed out ruefully.

The other couple had fallen in love while filming together on the island a couple of years previously. Madison had been the leading lady, Gideon the director of the film, a film that had won them both Oscars the following year. Consequently the two of them had great affection for the Isle of Man and had bought a home here, which they visited often with their now six-month-old daughter, Keilly.

'She may be,' Jonathan McGuire grated harshly. 'But I specifically asked Gideon—'

'Look,' Tory cut in quietly, aware they were still being

overheard, 'I suggest we go across to my car and continue this conversation there?' She raised dark brows.

He shot the receptionist an irritated look before turning on his heel without another word and walking over to the trolley that contained his luggage, which he had left parked at the bottom of some stairs.

Tory gave the receptionist a rueful shrug of her shoulders before following him, noting as she did so that as well as a suitcase there was a guitar case on the trolley Jonathan McGuire now pushed towards the automatically opening exit doors.

'Do you play?' she asked interestedly, falling into step at his side as they walked towards the car park. It was just as well that she had always walked fast herself; it took two of her strides to one of his much longer ones to keep up with him!

He looked at her blankly. 'Sorry?'

Tory somehow doubted that he was sorry at all, thought he was probably very rarely sorry for anything he did. But obviously someone had at least taught him some manners. 'I couldn't help noticing the guitar case.' She nodded towards it.

He continued to look at her with those expressionless grey eyes. 'So?'

Tory drew in a deep breath. 'Look, Mr McGuire, I suggest that the two of us start again.' She came to an abrupt halt on the pavement. 'My name is Tory Buchanan.' She held out her hand. 'I'm very pleased to welcome you to the Isle of Man.'

Jonathan McGuire still looked blankly at the slenderness of her hand for several long seconds, and then he slowly raised his own hand to grip hers. 'I've been to the island before,' he bit out economically, having released her hand after only the briefest of touches.

He had? Of course, she spent a lot of time away from the island herself, so it wasn't so surprising that she might have missed his visit. But, nevertheless, she had gained the impression on the telephone last night, as she'd spoken to Madison, that Jonathan McGuire wasn't familiar with the island, or the location of Madison and Gideon's house. In fact, that was the main reason Madison had asked if someone would be able to go to the airport to meet him.

His mouth twisted derisively. 'It was a very brief visit,' he drawled.

One he had no intention of talking about, his slightly challenging tone implied.

Well, that was okay; Tory had already decided that, good-looking as Jonathan McGuire might be, her favour towards Madison ended the moment she had dropped her brother off at the house! He was darkly cold and arrogant, when she had imagined him to be a golden-haired fun person, like Madison was herself. As far as Tory was concerned, Jonathan McGuire could keep his cold arrogance to himself!

'My car is parked over here.' She indicated they should turn to the left as they entered the car park. 'Actually, it's my father's,' she explained as she unlocked the back of the Land Rover, slightly muddy from where her father drove it around the fields that made up his farm. 'My mother and father have taken the car today to attend a wedding this morning,' she somehow felt she had to add. Although why she should feel that way she had no idea; this man's ungrateful attitude meant she owed him no explanations.

She didn't offer to help as he lifted his luggage into the back, getting in behind the wheel as she waited for him to stroll round and get into the passenger seat beside her before starting the engine. Ten years old, the engine roared protestingly for a few seconds before settling down to its normal erratic clonking noise, and she accelerated the vehicle towards the exit.

'Weren't you invited?'

'Invited where?' Tory turned briefly from feeding her ticket into the machine at the exit, the barrier instantly lifting to allow them to drive out; as she had only arrived at the airport half an hour ago she hadn't had to pay a parking fee.

'To the wedding,' Jonathan McGuire continued, perfectly relaxed in the seat next to her.

So he had been listening, after all! 'I was,' she returned. 'But...?'

'But a friend asked me to do her a favour instead,' Tory said quickly, deliberately not looking at him as she concentrated on her driving.

She sensed him looking at her through narrowed lids, nonetheless. Well, let him look. She had been invited to the wedding, but when Madison had asked if someone could meet her brother at the airport and take him to the house, Tory had been only too happy to offer to be the one to do it. After all, it was Tory's mother's niece who was getting married. Admittedly, the bride was Tory's cousin too, but she could still go to the reception later this afternoon.

'I play.'

Tory gave him a brief, puzzled glance. She seemed to have missed something somewhere!

'The guitar,' he explained. 'You asked if I play. I do.'

'Ah.' She nodded her understanding. 'What sort of music do you play?' she continued interestedly.

There was a brief silence, causing Tory to glance at him once again. His closed expression told her she had—once more!—ventured into forbidden territory. The problem with this man was that every subject seemed to have the potential of an unexplored minefield!

'Usually whatever I feel like playing,' he rasped dismissively.

Tory sighed at the deliberate snub, turning her attention back to her driving. She had only been trying to make polite conversation, for goodness' sake. Obviously a nicety wasted on Jonathan McGuire.

Only another half an hour or so and she could deposit him at his sister's home—and hopefully not see him again for the remainder of his visit. She just hoped he made it another brief one!

She tried to remember the little Madison had said about her brother during their call the previous evening. Madison had called him 'Jonny'; she remembered that. Tory couldn't ever imagine calling this remotely cold man by such an intimately friendly name!

But she could see that he looked wealthy enough; his clothes were obviously of good quality, and she could tell at a glance that his case and the guitar case were the best that money could buy. And, as Madison's brother, he must also be son of Susan Delaney—a woman had become an acting legend in her own lifetime, and a woman Tory had met several times and liked immensely, when she'd visited Madison and Gideon on the island. Perhaps Jonathan McGuire took after his father—because he was certainly nothing like his charming sister and mother!

Tory decided to forget about her less-than-gracious passenger and enjoy the drive instead. It was a lovely day, the early June weather warm and sunny, wild garlic, blue- and whitebells still in flower along the roadside, the vivid yellow-orange of the gorse so bright against fresh green foliage that it almost hurt the eyes to look at it.

Not even the taciturn Jonathan McGuire could spoil her enjoyment of a beautiful day like today!

As they approached the end of the long stretch of road, with the leaves of the trees either side of the road meeting overhead like a green arch, she automatically raised her hand.

'Hi, fairies,' the man at her side murmured softly.

Tory turned to look at him, blue eyes wide with surprise. He *had* been here before.

They had just driven over the Fairy Bridge, marked by a white wall either side of the road. It was considered bad luck not to show the 'little people' who lived under the bridge due respect by saying hello to them.

Perhaps Jonathan McGuire felt in need of good luck...?

Damn it, she was starting to feel intrigued by the man, in spite of herself. He was American, for one thing; what did a single American male, of only thirty-two or thirty-three, want from a small community like the Isle of Man? Beautiful as the island was, almost crime-free too, with a population of less than eighty thousand, it certainly couldn't be considered a fashionable holiday spot for single thirty-odd-year-old males!

She knew the same could be said of a young woman of only twenty-four as well, but it was completely different in her own case. She had been born here; her family were all here. Whereas Jonathan McGuire seemed to be getting away from his own family!

Yes, she *was* intrigued!

That was the last thing she wanted at the moment. She had come back home to do some thinking herself, to make some decisions of her own. She certainly didn't need a man like the remote Jonathan McGuire in that already complicated equation.

'I see you're aware of some of the quainter island traditions,' she remarked conversationally.

'I did tell you I had been here before,' he bit out, staring uninterestedly out of the window at his side.

She really didn't know why she was bothering. She—

'What the hell was that?' Jonathan McGuire gave a shocked gasp as a streak of red shot noisily past the Land Rover.

Tory smiled, completely unperturbed. 'Obviously you aren't aware of all the island traditions,' she drawled mockingly as another blaze of colour shot past them, blue this time, and if anything noisier than the red one. 'Ever heard of the TT Races? The Tourist Trophy?' she enlarged dryly.

She had been starting to wonder, despite his rather jaded behaviour, if perhaps the races could be the reason he was here, his completely unreadable expression told her that it wasn't.

Jonathan McGuire was frowning darkly. 'I take it those—motorbikes have something to do with that?'

'They certainly do.' Tory couldn't hold back her smile any longer. 'And I'm afraid you've chosen to visit the island at the beginning of Race Week.'

'I know I'm going to regret this,' he admitted with obvious reluctance, 'but what is Race Week? In fact, what is the Tourist Trophy?'

'Motorbike racing. The main races are next week,' she told him happily, completely unconcerned as several more motorbikes overtook them at blurringly fast speeds.

TT Fortnight, as the practice week and race week were generally known, had been taking place on the island for almost a hundred years, and while a lot of inhabitants still found it intrusive on their usual peace and quiet, Tory actually loved the atmosphere of those two weeks, when forty to fifty thousand people, usually accompanied by at least twenty-five thousand motorbikes, literally invaded the island, all intent on having fun and enjoying the racing.

'Not today?' Jonathan McGuire said.

'Oh, they haven't started racing yet today,' Tory assured him.

'You could have fooled me!' he muttered disgustedly.

She smiled. 'They close the roads off when the races are actually taking place.'

'They race on the roads?' He was obviously amazed at the idea.

Tory grinned. 'Not over the whole island, obviously—'

'Oh, obviously,' Jonathan responded. 'Madison didn't tell me about this.' He scowled once more.

'Madison isn't supposed to know you're here—remember?' Tory couldn't help returning wryly.

There was a brief silence. 'Touché, Miss Buchanan,' he finally drawled admiringly.

'Tory,' she instantly came back, surprised he had actually remembered her name; he had given the impression of being completely uninterested in anything outside himself. But perhaps she was being unfair to him... 'As we're going to be neighbours for a while...'

Those already flinty grey eyes iced over. 'I have no intention of socialising during my stay here,' he grated.

Tory drew in a sharp breath at his rudeness, instantly regretting her impulse to be friendly. 'I don't think I said I intended inviting you to a party—Mr McGuire,' she snapped coldly. Or, indeed, to anything else!

Another twenty minutes or so and she could say goodbye to this—this arrogant bastard. It couldn't pass soon enough for her!

She had intended taking him the scenic route through Douglas, along the promenade, where the horse trams travelled backwards and forwards every few minutes, and where the electric tram began its journey up to the north of the island to its final destination, Snaefell, the only mountain the island boasted.

But after the last few seconds' conversation he could jolly well take the less attractive route, past the Grandstand, along through Onchan, and then out towards Laxey! She was in no mood herself to play the gracious hostess and point out the places of interest.

She hadn't particularly wanted to go to her cousin Denise's wedding, had welcomed this excuse not to have to actually attend the service. But if she had known how uncommunicative—in fact positively rude!—the alternative was going to be, then she would have opted for attending the wedding!

'I've never seen so many bikes in one place,' Jonathan McGuire remarked incredulously as they drove past the Grandstand, with row upon row of the powerful machines parked there as the race fans gathered just to soak in the atmosphere before the race this afternoon.

'I shouldn't worry,' Tory told him abruptly. 'Madison and Gideon's house is well away from any of the roads, and my mother went shopping this morning, so you should have enough food that you won't need to go out again for some time if you don't want to.' And, after what he had said, she was sure he wouldn't want to!

Again there was a brief silence before Jonathan McGuire answered her. 'That was very kind of your mother.'

Tory's mouth tightened at his surprise at such a gesture from a complete stranger. 'She's a very kind woman. Besides,' she continued levelly, 'we're all very fond of Madison and Gideon. And Keilly is adorable,' she added affectionately.

'Yes, she is, isn't she?' he agreed huskily.

It was the first time during their acquaintance—very brief

acquaintance!—that Tory had heard anything like softness in his tone. But then, how could anyone, least of all her uncle, not be enchanted by the beautiful golden-haired Keilly?

'Not far to go now,' she realised with satisfaction, leaving Onchan behind them and driving out into the countryside once again.

She always felt refreshed, renewed, when she spent time on the island; there was a feeling of having time stand still. At the moment, with important decisions in front of her, that was something she desperately needed.

Unlike the arrogantly rude Jonathan McGuire, who was definitely something she didn't need!

'This is a very beautiful island.'

Tory was becoming used to his sudden, seemingly unconnected statements, and didn't even bother to look at him this time. 'It is,' she agreed.

'What work do you do here?'

She stiffened slightly. For a man who obviously didn't like personal questions himself, he was becoming a little too curious about her own life.

She shrugged. 'Running a farm is a full-time family concern,' she answered evasively.

Dressed as she was, in a light blue tee shirt and faded denims, the latter mud-spattered from where it had rained the day before, her face bare of make-up, she definitely had the look of someone straight off the farm.

The fact that farming wasn't what she did was none of this man's business.

'I suppose it is,' he responded, before once again turning to look out of the window.

It seemed that pleasantries were over for the day!

'What work do you do, Mr McGuire?' she prompted lightly.

'My family is in casinos in Reno.'

That was about as helpful as her own remark about farming being a full-time family concern—it actually told her precisely nothing!

'We have a casino on the island,' she said in friendly reply. 'Perhaps you would like to see it while you're here?' Although she couldn't imagine why; it was a completely soulless place, and the people who went there seemed to be either curious tourists or hardened gamblers—neither of which particularly interested Tory.

'Are you asking me out after all, Tory?' He raised mocking dark brows.

She gave him a startled glance, relaxing slightly as she saw the laughter lurking in dark grey eyes. So the man did have a sense of humour, after all!

'No, I'm not,' she assured him ruefully. 'Casinos hold no appeal for me, I'm afraid,' she added slightly apologetically. After all, it was his family business.

'Me neither,' he rejoined, that brief show of humour completely gone.

Tory waited for him to continue, and when he didn't she decided that had to be the end of that subject, too.

In the circumstances, it had been rather an odd thing to say. But then Jonathan McGuire, she was quickly coming to realise, was an enigma.

'Here we are,' she said with a certain amount of relief a few minutes later as she turned the Land Rover down the Tarmacked driveway that led to the Byrne house.

Even though she had lived in the adjoining farm most of her life, Tory could still appreciate the beauty of this particular spot, high up in the hills, completely away from everything and everyone, though the village of Laxey, with its huge black and red waterwheel, was still visible down in the valley.

The Byrne home had been the original farmhouse once—
it and the adjoining acre of land having been purchased
from Tory's parents a year ago. The house was now completely refurbished, looking splendidly grand in the sunlight, its pale lemon and white paint gleaming brightly.

Tory parked the vehicle in front of the house before getting down onto the Tarmac to go round and drop the tail-
board, relieved the journey was over at last. With any luck
she wouldn't have to see Jonathan McGuire again.

He put his bag and the guitar case down before turning
to look at her. 'I'm sorry I haven't been very good company,' he told her gruffly. 'My only excuse is that I wasn't
expecting anyone at the airport to meet me.'

Which was no excuse. Madison had taken the trouble to
call them the evening before, obviously concerned as to her
brother's comfort. Tory's mother had been shopping for
him this morning. And Tory herself had taken time out to
go and collect him.

'Do you have a key?' she prompted briskly, reaching into
her denims' pocket for the spare Madison and Gideon always left with her parents when they were away.

Jonathan McGuire reached into his own denims' pocket
and pulled out a duplicate silver key. 'Compliments of
Gideon,' he offered lazily.

'Fine.' She put her own key back in her pocket. 'If
there's anything else you need, I'm sure my parents would
be only too pleased to help.' She gestured across the neighbouring field to the white farmhouse and accompanying
barns and sheds that could be seen in the distance.

He reached out and grasped her arm as she would have
turned away and got back into the Land Rover. 'But not
you?' He demanded.

Tory was very aware of that hand on the bareness of her
arm, the skin warm and firm to the touch. She looked up

at him with dark blue eyes, shaking her head, her shaggy dark mane of hair moving softly against her shoulders. 'I may not be here. Like you, I'm only visiting.'

He frowned. 'But I thought you said—'

'You'll find food in the fridge, and bread in the bin.' She knew that because, although her mother had done the shopping, Tory had actually brought it over to the house and unpacked it. 'There's also one of my mother's apple pies in the cupboard.' She pulled out of his grasp, stepping lightly back into the Land Rover, anxious to be on her way now. 'The car is parked in the garage round the back of the house; the keys are hanging up next to the fridge. Oh, and Madison always leaves a list of relevant telephone numbers next to the phone.' She turned on the ignition, reaching out to close the door behind her.

Jonathan McGuire also reached out to grasp the door, preventing it from closing. 'Is yours there?' he asked softly. *Now* he decided to start being charming! Well, charm she had had, in plenty—and she certainly didn't want or need it from this man!

Her pointed chin rose challengingly. 'My parents' number is there, if you should need it.'

His head tilted to one side as he gave her a considering look. 'I haven't been very polite to you, have I...?'

Tory met his gaze unblinkingly for several seconds. 'No,' she finally replied.

Jonathan McGuire did blink, and when he raised his lids again that earlier humour was gleaming there once more. 'Tell me, do you get on well with my sister Madison?'

'Very,' she confirmed evenly.

'I thought you might.' He grinned suddenly.

It was like looking at a different person, Tory realised with a startled jolt. He looked years younger now he wasn't scowling grimly, his teeth white and even against his tanned skin, laughter lines crinkling beside his mouth and eyes—eyes that had now taken on a silver sheen rather than that flinty grey.

Tory wrenched her gaze away from his. 'I really do have to go now, Mr McGuire.' She pulled pointedly on the door he still held, relieved when, after only the slightest of hesitations, he decided to let go of it, allowing her to slam it shut. She wound the window down beside her. 'Just one more thing. If you do intend using the car while you're here, I shouldn't go out anywhere tomorrow; it's Mad Sunday.'

'Mad what?' he questioned suspiciously.

'Sunday,' she repeated.

'Well, I realise it's Sunday,' he said slowly. 'But what's mad about it?'

Tory grinned herself now. 'You remember all those motorbikes you saw at the Grandstand earlier? Well,' she continued at his confirming nod, 'those bikes, and about twenty thousand more, will be circling the TT course tomorrow—with only the mountain road being one-way. Mad Sunday!'

She put the vehicle into gear, released the handbrake and accelerated away, her last glimpse of Jonathan McGuire as she glanced in the driving mirror the totally dazed look on his face.

She couldn't help smiling to herself. If Jonathan McGuire had come to the island for peace and quiet—and she had a definite feeling that he had!—then he had chosen the wrong week to do it.

And in her opinion, after the hard time he had given her, it couldn't have happened to a nicer person!

CHAPTER TWO

HER mood wasn't particularly improved when she got back to the farm to find that Rupert had left a message on the answer-machine!

The machine itself had been her gift to her parents the previous summer, mainly so that she could leave messages on it herself, no matter where she was or what time zone she might be in, ensuring that her parents would always know she was okay.

But Tory had it switched on most of the time when she was at home, enabling her to pick and choose which calls she wanted to take.

She most certainly would not have taken this one from Rupert!

She had specifically told him she did not want him to call her while she was here. But in his usual high-handed fashion he had taken absolutely no notice of her.

'Hello, darling,' his charming, educated voice greeted smoothly, enabling Tory to actually visualise him as he sat back in his brown leather chair, leather-shod feet up on the desk, looking immaculate in his designer-label suit and tailored shirt, silk tie knotted perfectly. 'Just wanted to see if you're ready to come home yet. We all miss you.'

Tory turned off the machine with a definitive click. Damn him, she *was* home. And as for missing her—!

Her mouth tightened. No doubt they *were* missing her, but Rupert especially; she had helped put those leather shoes on his feet, the designer-label suit and tailored shirt on his back. In fact, she was his main meal ticket.

Oh, hell!

She dropped down into one of the kitchen chairs, elbows on the oak table as she rested her chin on her hands. The last thing she wanted was to become bitter and twisted. But what was she going to do?

That was what she had come here a week ago to find out. She was nearer the answer, she realised, she knew what she wanted to do. But if she did it all hell was going to break loose. She—

'Give us a hand, would you, love?' her father puffed as he pushed open the kitchen door, arm around her mother's waist as he helped her badly limping form into the room.

Tory jumped concernedly to her feet, rushing over to her mother's other side so the two of them could guide her over to one of the kitchen chairs. Her mother's left ankle was tightly bandaged; a pained expression was on her face.

'What on earth happened?' Tory gasped once they had her mother safely settled in the chair.

'I fell over coming out of the church.' Her mother was the one to answer, self-disgustedly, looking very summery in her floral pink and white suit with matching pink hat.

'And not a drop had passed her lips!' Tory's father, barely five feet six in height, his face ruddily weathered by the sun and wind, grinned his relief at having got back home without further mishap.

'Vanity, that's what did it. I should never have worn these high-heeled shoes,' her mother said heavily, giving the offending white shoes a glare—the one still on her foot and the other held in her hand—obviously very annoyed with herself for having fallen over in the first place. 'I don't remember when I last wore shoes like this. We've been stuck at the hospital the last half-hour while they X-rayed my ankle. Nothing's broken, thank goodness, but it's a nasty sprain.'

'I'll get you both a cup of tea,' Tory offered concernedly, Rupert's call forgotten in the face of this family crisis.

No matter how much her father might be smiling with affection at her mother's clumsiness, it *was* a crisis. Her mother was as much an essential part of running the farm as her father was, and now that she was no longer mobile...

'Good idea, love,' her father replied, also sitting down at the kitchen table now.

The whole family spent a lot of time in this room. All of their meals were eaten around this table, and they often lingered here, after they had cleared away in the evenings, to just sit and chat.

'How did the wedding go?' Tory moved swiftly around the room making the tea.

Her mother's expression instantly softened, her face as weathered by the elements as her husband's, but rounder, as was her plump body. 'Beautiful.' She smiled reminiscently. 'I do love a good wedding.'

'Denise looked well enough,' her father added less enthusiastically, obviously uncomfortable in the shirt and suit he had been persuaded into wearing for the occasion. 'Although I still can't say I'm too keen on that young man she's married.'

'Wait until it's your turn, Tory.' Her mother gave her a knowing look. 'No man is going to be good enough for you, either!'

'You have that about right, Thelma,' Tory's father agreed gruffly. 'Because no man *is* good enough for our Tory!'

Tory gave them both an affectionate smile as she handed them their cups of tea. 'I wouldn't worry about that too much if I were you; I don't intend marrying for years yet.' If ever!

Not that she had always felt that way. Until a short time

ago she had had the same hopes and dreams as other women her age: a husband, children, a warm family home like the one she had grown up in.

But that had all changed now.

As had Rupert. But too late—fortunately! After years of saying marriage wasn't for him, Rupert had suddenly done an about-face a few weeks ago, and now urged her to marry him every opportunity he had.

Maybe if he had felt that way a few years ago Tory would have accepted, she acknowledged. But not any more. Rupert was no longer a golden-haired god to her. In fact, as she now knew only too well, he had feet of clay. She just thanked goodness he hadn't asked her to marry him a couple of years ago; then she would have made the biggest mistake of her life by accepting him!

'Well, I'm glad the wedding went well.' She smiled. 'Although it's a shame about your ankle, Mum.'

'My own fault,' her mother dismissed. 'How did you get on with Madison's brother Jonny?' she asked interestedly.

Tory grimaced as she sat down at the table with her own cup of tea. 'If I tell you I still called him Mr McGuire when I dropped him off at the house—' and dropping him off a cliff might have been a better idea! '—perhaps that will tell you how well I got on with him!'

'Oh, dear,' her mother responded worriedly. 'And the Byrnes are such a nice couple.'

International film star and director they might be, Oscar winners at that, and Madison's mother the world-renowned actress Susan Delaney and Gideon's late father the English actor, John Byrne—having been as famous himself before his early death thirty or so years ago—but to Tory's parents, Madison and Gideon were just 'the Byrnes'.

The island was home to several actors, a well-known television chef, several famous musicians and singers, as well as a handful of successful writers, amongst several lesser known millionaires. The islanders just took it in their stride if they happened to find themselves standing next to one of them in the till queue at the supermarket! After all, they all had to eat, too.

'I didn't—' She broke off abruptly as the telephone began to ring.

Damn—she had forgotten to switch the answer-machine back on after listening to Rupert's message earlier. And it didn't need two guesses to know that it would be Rupert calling again.

Damn, damn, damn!

'Would you like me to get that?' her father offered gently as he saw the displeased look on her face.

Coming back here to give herself room to think was one thing. Letting her father fight her battles for her was something else entirely.

'It's okay.' She stood up, snatching up the receiver. 'Yes?' she snapped uncompromisingly.

There was a brief pause on the other end of the line, before, 'How did you know it was me?'

Not Rupert! 'I didn't,' she answered Jonathan McGuire in a slightly sheepish voice, turning away from the curious glances of her parents in the hope that they wouldn't see her uncomfortable blush.

'Who else has upset you today?' he mused mockingly, that American drawl even more distinct over a telephone line.

'No one in particular,' she said brightly. What did he want? He had left her in no doubt when she parted from him an hour ago that he wanted to be left alone.

'You're very good at that, aren't you?' he said admiringly.

Tory hesitated. 'At what?'

'The evasive answer,' he came back instantly.

She gave a startled laugh. 'And that coming from the expert at evasive answers!' She knew less about Jonathan McGuire after spending almost forty minutes in his company than she had before she met him!

A throaty chuckle resounded down the telephone line. 'Okay, so you aren't going to tell me who else has upset you today,' he accepted. 'I won't keep you long,' he added more briskly, 'I know you must be anxious to go to your cousin's wedding. I—that's actually the reason I'm phoning.'

Tory blinked. 'You aren't suggesting you would like to come with me?' she said disbelievingly.

She could just imagine the family speculation if she arrived at her cousin Denise's wedding reception with a tall, dark American in tow! Not that she intended going at all now that her mother and father weren't going to be there, but surely Jonathan McGuire couldn't be—

'Hell, no!' he instantly disabused her of that illusion. 'I—having had time to—think about things—I realise I owe you an apology for my behaviour earlier—'

'I thought you had already made one,' Tory said guardedly.

'For not thanking you for taking time out of your day to pick me up at the airport,' he completed determinedly. 'I—thank you.'

Ouch, she bet that hurt.

'You're welcome,' she returned lightly.

There was a deep sigh at the other end of the line. 'I'm not usually as rude as I was today—'

'Don't tell me—you're usually ruder!' she teased.

'You aren't making this easy for me, are you,' he responded irritably.

Well, she wasn't sure what 'this' was...! He had apologised, she had accepted that apology, so what was he still doing on the line?

'Do you think I should?' she returned warily.

After all, everything he had said was true; she had taken time out of her day, missed her cousin's wedding, just so that she could go to the airport and pick him up. Only to be faced with his rude uncooperativeness. The fact that she had been glad of the excuse not to go to the wedding was irrelevant.

'Probably not,' he accepted with resignation. 'When you see your mother could you also thank her for the pie? I was hungry when I got here, so I've already eaten a piece; it's delicious.'

It certainly was, her mother was one of the best pastry-makers on the island. Luckily Tory seemed to have a metabolism that could handle her mother's wonderful cooking, which didn't just stop at pastry, otherwise she might have ended up a very chubby child and an even fatter adult!

'Why don't you tell her yourself?' Tory declared, suddenly seeing a way of ending this conversation without appearing rude herself. 'She's sitting right here.' She held the receiver out to her mother before Jonathan McGuire could make any response—positive or negative—to her suggestion.

Tory moved to kiss her father lightly on the cheek. 'I'm just popping over to the studio for a while,' she told him softly. 'Give me a yell if you need me for anything,' she added with a glance towards her mother, the pleased flush to her mother's cheeks as she listened to Jonathan McGuire telling Tory that he must be repeating his praise of her mother's pastry.

Tory gave a smile as she left the farmhouse. The way to a man's heart might be through his stomach, but the way to her mother's was to show appreciation for her cooking.

It looked as if Jonathan McGuire was succeeding in charming one member of the Buchanan family at least.

Her smiled faded as she crossed the yard and entered the outhouse that her father had allowed her to convert into a studio. She stopped just inside the door, looking around her, feeling— What...? Everywhere she looked there was evidence of her success. And once that had been all she wanted. She had left the island six years ago in search of that dream. But after five years at the top she had realised it wasn't enough. She wanted more.

She had taken a risk six years ago, put all her hopes in her own ability, and she had been successful. Did she now have the courage, while still at the top, to take a sideways step in that career?

Rupert thought she was mad even to consider taking the step that had consumed her thoughts over the last few months. But then Rupert had his own reasons for keeping her exactly where she was, doing what she was doing. It suited his own agenda.

But did it still suit hers?

If she knew the answer to that then she wouldn't still be here on the island.

She wouldn't have had to meet the rudely taciturn Jonathan McGuire today either!

'Arrogant. Self-interested. Inconsiderate!' Tory muttered to herself as she checked the contents of the saucepans bubbling away on top of the Aga.

'Bad sign that, love,' her father observed as he came into the kitchen from outside, back in his comfortable work clothes today, looking much more at ease. 'Talking to yourself,' he explained at Tory's questioning look.

She made a face. 'Lunch should be ready in fifteen minutes.'

That was the reason she was talking to herself. Oh, not because, as her mother was incapacitated, she was the one actually cooking the Sunday lunch; she had always been happy to do her share of work about the farm, easily fell back into doing that when she was home.

No, cooking lunch wasn't the problem—it was the fact that Jonathan McGuire was invited to eat it that was irritating her!

He had given her every indication yesterday that he was doing a Greta Garbo—wanted to be alone—and yet before he had finished talking to her mother on the telephone the previous day he had accepted an invitation to come to Sunday lunch.

Tory had been all for eating in the kitchen as they usually did, but her mother had insisted that they open up the rarely used dining room at the back of the house in honour of their guest.

Honour!

Tory didn't feel in the least honoured. Sunday lunch was always an especially enjoyable family occasion, with the afternoon spent relaxing in front of the television or reading the newspapers. If eating in the dining room was an example of how this Sunday was going to go, then her father could forget about his television and Tory her newspapers; neither was allowed when they had guests. Their only hope was that this guest wouldn't linger long after lunch!

She couldn't even begin to imagine what had made Jonathan McGuire accept the invitation in the first place. So much for his claim that he didn't intend socialising while he was here!

She gave an impatient glance at her wristwatch. 'If our guest doesn't arrive soon, he's going to miss lunch altogether,' she muttered irritably.

'I'm sure—' Her father broke off what he had been about

to say as the sound of a vehicle arriving outside in the yard could clearly be heard. 'Talk of the devil.' He grinned. 'I had better go up and get some clean clothes on, at least.' He looked down ruefully at his muddy working overalls. 'Or your mother won't be too happy with me!' He was whistling as he left the room to go upstairs.

With her mother lying down in the sitting room, resting her ankle until lunch was ready, and her father upstairs changing, it was left to Tory to go in answer to the ringing of the front doorbell. A rarely used front doorbell! It was much more friendly in this island community to use the side or back door.

It took Tory several minutes to pull back the heavy bolts at the top and bottom of the door, before using the key to unlock it, and the hinges creaked from lack of use when she finally managed to open it.

'You don't have the Fort Knox gold in there, do you?' Jonathan McGuire drawled, obviously having heard the grating of the bolts and unlocking of the door.

At least, Tory assumed it was him; most of him seemed to be hidden behind a large bunch of yellow chrysanthemums wrapped in tissue paper, only his long denim-clad legs revealed beneath them.

'Very funny,' Tory snapped, stepping back to let him inside. 'But for future reference, could you use the back door?' she added with pointed sarcasm as she went through the drawn-out process of replacing the bolts and turning the lock.

The chrysanthemums were slowly lowered to reveal Jonathan McGuire's handsome face. 'Sorry,' he grimaced.

He didn't look either as tired, or grim, as he had yesterday. In fact, he looked dangerously attractive, Tory decided, the darkness of his hair still damp from a recent shower and inclined to curl, those grey eyes warm, the sculptured mouth smiling.

Tory didn't give him an answering smile. 'This way,' she told him abruptly, leading the way down the hallway back to the kitchen.

They might be going to eat in the dining room soon, but for the moment he would have to put up with the informality of the kitchen; she couldn't play hostess to him *and* cook the meal any other way!

'You really shouldn't have bothered, Mr McGuire.' She nodded in the direction of the flowers he still held; he must have called in to the shop in the village this morning.

'Er—I'm afraid they aren't for you,' he admitted. 'They're for your mother; my own mother told me to always take flowers to give to my hostess.'

How to feel small in one easy lesson!

'I'm sure my mother will be thrilled,' Tory replied, her cheeks flushed with embarrassment now. That would teach her not to try to be clever!

'These are for you.' He reached into his jacket pocket and pulled out a box of chocolates. 'Flowers for the hostess, chocolates for the daughter.' He gave a rueful shrug at this second lesson in good manners obviously taught to him by his mother.

As peace offerings went, it was a very small box of chocolates. But it had the advantage of being her favourite brand.

'Thank you,' Tory accepted, their fingers lightly touching as she took the box from him.

Ouch!

Something like an electric shock made her hand tingle, before it travelled up her arm, the feeling slowly defusing but leaving her feeling slightly breathless.

What was *that*?

She shook her head before turning to put the chocolates down on the side. 'Can I offer you a drink before lunch, Mr McGuire?' she enquired, still slightly dizzied by her reaction to just the briefest touch of his fingers against hers.

He gave no indication of being so affected himself, putting the flowers down on the table to reveal he once again wore a jacket and shirt with his denims, the jacket black this time, the shirt light blue.

'If you're having a drink then I'll join you,' he said. 'On the condition you stop calling me Mr McGuire—Tory.'

'Jonathan,' she bit out, accompanied by a terse nod of her head. There was no way she could call him Jonny! 'We have sherry, or there's a bottle of white wine cooling in the fridge. I hope you like chicken.'

For all she knew he could be a vegetarian—although it would be singularly stupid on his part not to have mentioned that fact to her mother on the telephone the previous day.

'Love it.' He had opened the fridge door and taken out the bottle of white wine. 'Do you have a corkscrew for this?'

'Make yourself at home, why don't you?' Tory mumbled to herself as she searched through the drawer for the corkscrew, turning to check the vegetables again as he opened the bottle and poured some wine into two of the glasses sitting on the side.

'Mr McGuire,' her father greeted him a few seconds later as he came into the kitchen, holding out his hand. 'Dan Buchanan. Come through to the sitting room and meet my wife. Everything okay with you, Tory?' He quirked questioning brows.

Fine—now that he had come down to take over entertaining their guest! 'I'll give you a shout when I've served the meal,' she said.

Jonathan gave her a quick glance. 'I hope I haven't put you to too much trouble on my behalf...?'

'Not in the least,' Tory assured him airily. 'We were having a roast lunch anyway,' she told him, knowing by the narrowing of those silver-grey eyes that Jonathan McGuire, at least, hadn't missed the intended slight.

'I'm afraid my wife fell over yesterday and sprained her ankle,' her father told their guest. 'But Tory cooks almost as well as her mother.'

'Almost?' Tory deliberately rose to her father's teasing; it was part of what she most enjoyed about being at home. Her parents were such genuine down-to-earth people. Unlike the crowd she was surrounded by in London!

'The proof will be in the eating.' Her father gave Jonathan a conspiratorial wink. 'Let's go through, Jonathan, and say hello to Thelma; she's been looking forward to meeting you.'

Which put her mother in the minority as far as Tory was concerned. Gifts of flowers and chocolates did not alter the fact that the man was incredibly rude.

Although there was no sign of that rudeness as the four of them sat down to lunch, her mother helped into the dining room by Jonathan McGuire's solicitous hand under her elbow.

Probably another lesson in manners taught him by his mother, Tory decided disgruntledly.

Now who was being rude and uncooperative?

So she was. But she just couldn't get past the man she had met yesterday. Even if Jonathan's next words did make it seem that he was determined to wipe out that image to-day...

'This is delicious,' he told her after tasting the succulent chicken and accompanying vegetables. He was seated next to Tory at the table, her parents facing them. 'School

Sunday lunches were never as good as this!' he commented. 'I grew up believing English cooking had to be the worst in the world!'

Tory's brows rose over surprised blue eyes. 'You went to school in England?' How strange, when his parents were both American.

He met her gaze steadily for several long seconds. 'English education, paradoxically, is the best in the world,' he finally answered.

'And your parents obviously wanted the best for you,' she acknowledged sardonically.

His eyes narrowed speculatively for several seconds before he turned to her mother. 'I had no idea when I accepted your invitation yesterday, Thelma, that you had hurt your ankle, that it would be Tory I was making extra work for,' he said.

If he was trying to make her feel guilty, then he was succeeding!

Though if she were truthful with herself, it wasn't really Jonathan she was annoyed with today. Rupert had telephoned again this morning, shortly before the other man arrived, annoying her intensely with his certainty that she would be back in London soon, ready to begin another round of work and mindless parties.

'It really was no trouble,' she assured Jonathan awkwardly; after all, he was her parents' guest, and she really wasn't being very welcoming. 'I'm glad you're enjoying it. There's one of Mum's cherry pies for dessert,' she added.

'If I'm not careful I shall be putting on weight while I'm here,' he came back satirically.

Tory doubted that very much. Jonathan had the build of an athlete, without looking muscle-bound—something she found most unattractive in a man.

Not that she wanted to find Jonathan McGuire attractive!

She was having enough trouble trying to sort her own life out, without complicating it with an attraction that was going nowhere. Not that Jonathan had given any indication that he found her in the least attractive anyway!

Could she possibly be a bit irritated with him because of that, too?

Maybe, she conceded. Although she never made anything of her looks when she was at home, always wore denims and tee shirts for convenience's sake—she never knew when her father was going to ask her to go and help him on the farm. And she never bothered with make-up when she was here, either; it was a relief not to always have to look perfect.

But, even so, Jonathan McGuire hadn't given any indication that he had even noticed she was female, let alone an attractive one!

'How are Madison and Gideon?' her mother asked interestedly. 'And the adorable Keilly, of course,' she added indulgently.

'I can see my niece has been breaking hearts this side of the Atlantic, too,' Jonathan recognised. 'Maddie and Gideon are fine. They're visiting Maddie's godfather and his wife at the moment; Edgar and Claire have a four-month-old son. Actually, I believe Claire is Manx,' he continued thoughtfully. 'Her name was Christian before she married Edgar,' he explained helpfully.

'A good Manx name,' Tory's father said approvingly.

'So I believe,' Jonathan replied. 'It's the name they've given the baby.'

'I can't say we know a Claire Christian…do we, Thelma?' Tory's father said.

'Sorry.' Her mother smiled apologetically. 'I expect your parents are thrilled about little Keilly, aren't they? Is it their first grandchild?'

'They are. And it is. So far...' Jonathan confirmed dryly.

Tory gave him a thoughtful glance. Her own parents might not think any man was good enough to marry her, but that didn't stop them wanting grandchildren of their own. Could Jonathan's parents, now that they had one grandchild, possibly be putting the same emotional pressure on him? Probably, she decided. It seemed to be the way with parents that they wanted to see their children happily settled.

Although if Jonathan had reached the age of thirty-two or thirty-three without succumbing to matrimony, and he had come alone on his visit to the island, it didn't look as if it was a possibility in the near future!

'And Gideon's parents?' her mother continued happily. 'I expect they're thrilled, too?'

Jonathan's expression didn't change, and yet Tory felt other, subtle changes in him as he sat next to her, his body tense now, a certain wariness in his eyes.

Because her mother had mentioned Gideon's parents? Or because she had mentioned Gideon himself? Did the two men not get on?

She found the latter hard to believe. The two men were very alike. Gideon was also forceful, very self-possessed—like this man, to the point of arrogance. Or perhaps Jonathan just didn't think Gideon was good enough for Madison? Tory believed older brothers could be like that, too.

Not that Tory had any siblings of her own, older or younger, but she could imagine Jonathan being quite protective of his 'little sister'...

'Gideon's parents are both dead,' Jonathan finally answered harshly, putting his knife and fork down on his almost empty plate. 'And now I really think I should be going; I've interrupted your Sunday afternoon for long enough,' he added, with what seemed to Tory a deliberately forced softening of his tone.

Her mother looked surprised. 'But we haven't had dessert yet,' she protested with light rebuke.

Tory knew only too well, no one was allowed to leave without eating her mother's desserts!

She stood up. 'Would you like to help me clear the plates, Jonathan?' she suggested. 'Then you can sample Mum's cherry pie and tell her which one you prefer—the apple or the cherry.' She smiled at her blushing mother.

Perhaps it wasn't quite the thing to do to ask the guest to help clear away, but it had seemed to Tory that Jonathan needed a brief respite from a conversation that seemed to be getting a little too personal for his liking. Or comfort!

Not that she could say what could possibly make him feel uncomfortable talking about his sister and her husband; she just knew that it was.

Unless it was just that he had had enough of their provincial company for one day. After all, being based in Reno, involved in the running of casinos, he would obviously be used to a much more sophisticated form of entertainment. And company!

'Thank you for that,' he said quietly once they reached the kitchen, putting the plates he carried down on the side.

Tory looked at the muscled width of his back as he stood turned away from her, once again wondering why a man like him had decided to bury himself on the Isle of Man for an indefinite period, and once again coming up with no answer!

Or perhaps, like her, he just needed some time and space to be able to think…?

Also, like her, he wasn't about to discuss what he was thinking about with a third party…

He turned sharply, as if sensing her puzzled gaze on him,

his expression immediately guarded. 'I meant, of course, for helping me avoid insulting your mother by missing out on dessert,' he explained.

Oh, sure he did! 'Of course,' she repeated dryly, still not absolutely sure of his reason for saying he was leaving a few minutes ago. If it was because she and her parents simply bored him, then he was rude! But, then, she had already known that, hadn't she?

He gave her a piercingly searching look, a look Tory withstood with calm indifference. He was wasting his time trying to disconcert her in that particular way; she was more than used to being in the spotlight.

Jonathan was the first one to break away from their locked gazes. 'Would you like me to carry anything through for you?' he offered distantly.

'The cream.' She opened the fridge and took the jug of cream out. 'Unless you would prefer ice-cream? I believe Americans prefer it with their dessert?'

During the last five years she had been to America at least a dozen times herself, and had always noticed this preference with pie. Although Jonathan McGuire probably thought she had just watched a lot of American pro-grammes on the television!

He gave a slight inclination of his head. 'You believe correctly,' he drawled.

She took the ice-cream from the freezer, carrying through that and the pie while Jonathan carried all the other things.

Her father turned to smile at them both as they came into the room. 'I was just saying to your mother, Tory; perhaps Jonathan would like you to take him out for a ride this afternoon?'

Tory gave her father an irritated frown. She did not want to spend any more time in Jonathan McGuire's company than she had to. Besides, he was their guest, not hers.

She wasn't daft; she knew exactly what her father was up to. There was a good war film on the television this afternoon, and her father didn't want to miss it! If he could manage to persuade Jonathan to go out with Tory, then he would be able to watch it.

Jonathan looked puzzled. 'But I thought you told me it was best to stay in this afternoon?' he reminded Tory. 'Something to do with the bikes on the TT course?' he added.

'Well, that's exactly what I'm talking about,' her father told him jovially. 'Tory hasn't been round the course herself for a couple of years; I'm sure she would love to take you. Wouldn't you love?' he pressed hopefully. 'It's an experience everyone should have once in their lifetime!' he assured Jonathan.

'You ride a motorbike?' Jonathan no longer looked puzzled—he looked astounded.

Tory bristled at his disbelieving expression. She had been born on the island, lived here all her life until six years ago, still spent as much time here as work and other commitments would allow, and motorbikes were a fact of the island, whether you liked them or not. Five years ago Tory had bought her own motorbike, on the basis that if you couldn't beat them, you joined them!

'Yes, I ride a motorbike,' she confirmed stiffly. 'I'll take you out on it when we've finished lunch. If you would like to go?'

If you dare! her tone implied.

CHAPTER THREE

'How ever did we get ourselves into this?' Jonathan exclaimed as she handed him the second helmet before leaving the house, the two of them striding across the yard to the shed where Tory kept her bike.

She had been wondering that herself all the time she was in her bedroom putting on her leathers, forgoing dessert herself to leave Jonathan downstairs with her parents to enjoy his.

But she knew exactly why she had behaved in the way that she had; Jonathan's scornful reaction to hearing she rode a motorbike had clearly indicated he didn't believe she was big enough to handle a pushbike, let alone a machine powerful enough to take the two of them around the TT course.

'Don't you know?' she derided, already starting to feel hot in the black leathers as the warm sun shone down on them.

Dark brows rose over grey eyes. 'Do you?'

Tory nodded grimly. 'You were dared into it—by me! And I was goaded into it—by you!'

Jonathan grimaced. 'Very commendable!' he responded mockingly. 'Just how long is this TT course?' he asked slowly.

'Almost thirty-eight miles.' She unlocked the shed, throwing back the doors.

'Thirty-eight—! I think maybe I should have forgone that second helping of pie your mother pressed on me!' he said with feeling.

Tory turned to chuckle softly at his expression. 'Frightened you might shortly see it again?'

'God, I hope not,' he groaned.

Tory went into the shed to get her bike, needing all her strength to push it outside into the yard, sparing Jonathan a brief glance from beneath lowered lashes once she had done so. She wasn't disappointed; he was staring open-mouthed at the powerful machine.

Bright red, with a 750cc engine, it was an extremely powerful, as well as beautiful, bike.

'Can you really ride that thing?' he queried suspiciously.

Her mouth tightened. Had he forgotten that it was exactly this sort of attitude that had got them into this in the first place? Obviously not a man who learnt his lesson the first time around!

She got on the leather seat, putting her helmet on before starting the powerful engine. 'Get on,' she told him firmly. 'We'll go down to the Grandstand where the races start from. And for goodness' sake, hold on!' she ordered warningly.

She held the bike steady as Jonathan got on behind her, tensing slightly as his arms curved about her waist. Well, she was the one who had told him to hold on!

But it wasn't too difficult once they were on the TT course itself, with the sun beating down, the breeze whistling past them, and with the comradeship of the other bikers, to almost forget she had Jonathan McGuire as a passenger. Only the occasional tightening of his grip about her waist reminded her.

She had forgotten the thrill of this ride too, felt totally exhilarated as the miles passed beneath them.

As they approached the Grandstand after the first lap of the circuit she felt a dig in her ribs, and turned slightly to see what Jonathan wanted, only to find him pointing towards the parking area where thousands of bikers were already gathered.

Disappointed, she throttled down before turning into an empty space and switching off the engine, taking off her helmet to shake her dark hair loose about her shoulders before turning to look at Jonathan.

A very green-looking Jonathan!

'Are you okay?' she gasped concernedly as he got off the bike, staggering slightly.

He ripped off his own helmet, taking in huge gulps of air now that he was back on *terra firma*. 'Do I look all right?' he snarled through gritted teeth.

Actually, he looked terrible, Tory decided as she swung off the bike too, putting it on its stand before turning back to him. 'I—'

'Tory! Hey, Tory!'

They both turned to the leather-clad figure limping towards them, a grin of pure pleasure splitting the ruggedly hewn features of the newcomer.

'Terry!' Tory greeted with equal pleasure before being gathered up into a bear hug.

'It's great to see you back on the island.' Terry moved back slightly to look down at her, still grinning. 'Back on the bike, too.' He nodded his approval 'We missed you here last year,' he said wistfully.

She grinned. 'Work commitments.'

Terry grinned back. 'How's it going?'

'Oh, you know—'

'I hate to interrupt this moving reunion—' the sarcasm in Jonathan's tone completely belied his words '—but could one of you point me in the direction of a public convenience?'

Terry gave Tory an 'is he with you?' look, before answering the other man. 'Over there, mate.' He waved in the direction of the Grandstand.

'Thank you.' Jonathan gave a terse nod, his face set in grim lines as he strode off in the direction indicated.

'Friend of yours?' Terry said meaningfully.

'Sort of,' Tory replied, watching Jonathan until he disappeared into the Gents. 'I don't think he's too impressed with our TT course,' she understated, not sure that Jonathan hadn't excused himself so that he could be sick! 'If he isn't back in ten minutes, perhaps you had better go and see if he's all right,' she suggested.

Terry chuckled. 'He's American, isn't he?'

'Mmm,' she confirmed vaguely, feeling slightly guilty that she hadn't realised Jonathan wasn't enjoying the ride as much as she was. 'How are Jane and the family?' She changed the subject as she turned back to Terry.

'All well,' he responded. 'We all missed you at the wedding yesterday.'

As her cousin—in fact, Denise's older brother—of course Terry and his family would also have been at the ceremony. 'I'm sorry I missed it, too,' she said, not altogether truthfully. 'But I had—other commitments.'

That 'commitment'—she was glad to see!—was making his way back to them through the crowd at this very moment, no longer looking quite as green as he had when Tory had first looked at him after their ride.

'How is Aunty Thelma today?' Terry enquired.

'Hobbling about,' Tory assured him, happier now that she knew Jonathan wasn't collapsed in a heap somewhere. 'You know Mum,' she opined, 'you can't keep her down for long!'

'That's true,' Terry acknowledged affectionately. 'I have to say,' he went on thoughtfully as he gave the approaching

Jonathan McGuire a glance, 'he's a definite improvement on the other one you brought home.'

The 'other one', Tory knew, being Rupert! But then Rupert, with his rakish London sophistication, on the one, never to be repeated occasion he had accompanied her to the island, hadn't set out to win any points for charm. He had been deliberately condescending, to her family and friends alike.

But, by the same token, Jonathan McGuire was not someone she had brought home!

'So, what do you think of our TT course?' Terry turned to ask the other man as he rejoined them, giving Tory no opportunity to refute her cousin's mistaken impression concerning her relationship to Jonathan.

Terry had always had a wicked sense of humour, Tory remembered with an inward groan. Admittedly Jonathan wasn't green any more, but he was certainly still very white.

'Jonathan McGuire. Terry Bridson.' She introduced the two men quickly as she saw that Jonathan's eyes were once again the flinty grey colour that warned of impending danger to anyone who crossed him, and Terry's teasing definitely came under that heading!

She watched as the two men shook hands, Terry still grinning, Jonathan managing a grimace of a smile in return.

'Your TT course is—interesting,' Jonathan ventured. 'What other forms of torture do you have for the unsuspecting tourist?'

The latter was added so mildly that the sarcasm underlying the remark didn't sink in with Tory for several seconds.

Terry, however, roared with laughter, slapping the other man companionably on the back. 'We call it fun here on the island.' He grinned.

'Hmm,' Jonathan responded non-committally. 'Are you one of the competitors?'

'Not any more.' Terry sobered. 'I came off a few years ago.' He slapped his damaged knee, the reason for his pronounced limp. 'I don't have the agility to be a competitor any more.'

'Much to his family's relief,' Tory put in firmly.

Terry shrugged. 'There is that, I suppose.' But the wistfulness could clearly be heard in his voice. 'Are you staying on the island long, Jonathan? Or are you just here for TT?'

From the look on his face, Jonathan didn't care if he never looked at another motorbike in his lifetime!

'I'm unsure of the length of my stay,' he answered the other man, that guarded tone back in his voice.

'If you're still here next week, maybe you and Tory would like to come out for a quiet drink.' Terry seemed completely oblivious to the other man's non-committal answer. 'This week is out, I'm afraid. For obvious reasons.' He looked about them, the noise of bike engines, chatter and laughter almost deafening.

So was next week, as far as Tory was concerned. She had no wish to be linked as the other half of a couple with Jonathan McGuire! Especially where her family was concerned.

'We had better be getting back.' She touched her cousin's arm in apology. 'And we'll take a raincheck on next week,' she added as she pulled her helmet back on. 'Neither of us is sure of our plans at the moment.'

'Fine,' Terry said. 'But give me a ring before you go back to London. Nice to meet you, Jonathan,' he finished, before limping back to the group of friends he had been talking with when they had arrived.

Tory looked at the still ashen-faced Jonathan. 'Do you

feel up to riding back to the farm on the bike? I promise I'll go slowly.'

He briefly shut his eyes and then opened them again as he pulled his own helmet back on. 'This has got to be the maddest thing I've ever done in my life,' he said.

She gave him a mischievous look. 'It beats hot-air ballooning, hang-gliding and parachuting!'

'I've never done any of those, either.'

'You haven't lived!' Tory told him with feeling, having done—and enjoyed—all three.

He looked at her, unimpressed. 'I'm only just beginning to realise that...' He climbed back on the pillion seat. 'I'll enjoy this if it kills me!' he announced determinedly.

She laughed, lifting up a hand in farewell to Terry and his friends, several of whom she recognised, before accelerating the bike back into the stream of other bikes—but heading towards the coastal road, away from the actual course.

Jonathan didn't have her in quite such a death-grip this time, and was much more relaxed behind her now, seeming to actually be enjoying the uninterrupted views of the Irish sea, the sheer cliffs rising up from it in places, the hillsides covered in the vivid yellow-orange gorse.

Tory didn't head straight back to the farm, taking the road into Laxey instead, going down the road that led to the beach. It was crowded of course, but the sun, the sand, the bracing sea air, were all quite invigorating.

'Come on, I'll buy you an ice-cream,' she told the no longer white-faced Jonathan once she had parked the bike, leaving their helmets locked to the side of the machine.

Jonathan shook his head a few minutes later as they walked along side by side, eating the vanilla ice-creams in their cornets. Dozens of people were milling about, either on the beach itself or walking along as they were. 'Maddie

and Gideon are never going to believe this. Gideon a̶ ̶ ̶ ̶d
me this is one of the most peaceful places on earth!'

'Fifty weeks of the year it is. Well…possibly a little less than that; we also have the Manx Grand Prix and the Southern One Hundred—also motorcycle races,' Tory told him ruefully. 'But by Monday of next week the majority of these people will have gone home.'

'Home where?' he questioned.

'Europe mostly, mainly Germany. But we get people from all over the world, including the States. Believe it or not, most of the bikers are actually accountants, lawyers, white collar workers; they just let their hair down on the Isle of Man for two weeks of the year. They just want to watch the races and in between have a good time,' she explained affectionately. 'For instance, it's going to be absolutely wild in Douglas this evening.'

'That's the capital, isn't it? Jonathan asked.

'It is now, but years ago it used to be Castletown.'

Jonathan looked at her over the top of his ice-cream. 'Were you issuing an invitation just now?' he murmured huskily.

Tory gave him a startled glance. An invitation—?

'To join in this evening's fun in Douglas,' Jonathan drawled at her puzzled expression.

Of course she hadn't been issuing an invitation! She was just very proud of her island home, wanted other people to love it as much as she did.

She should have known what sort of person Rupert was three years ago when he'd come here with her; he had absolutely hated the island, had called it a provincial wilderness!

'Or perhaps I should invite you as my guest,' Jonathan continued at her lack of response. 'It seems only fair as you've taken me out this afternoon.'

'Drive down in the car, you mean,' Tory said knowingly.

He gave a rueful smile. 'That's exactly what I mean!'

'And what happened to that not intending to socialise while you're here that you mentioned yesterday?' she reminded pointedly.

He had only been here a little over twenty-four hours, and so far he had been to her parents' home for lunch, been taken out for a bike ride by her, and now he was asking her to spend the evening with him, too.

But she did not want to go out with Jonathan this evening, or any other evening for that matter. She was no more interested in socialising than he had told her he was yesterday…especially not with him!

Why especially not with him…?

Oh, shut up, she told that inner voice crossly. It was obvious why not; the man was arrogant, rude, didn't belong here any more than Rupert did!

The latter might be true, she conceded slowly, but the arrogance and rudeness hadn't been as noticeable today…

'I really am sorry I was so rude and uncooperative yesterday,' Jonathan grated, seeming to pick up on at least some of her thoughts. 'My only excuse—and it really isn't good enough—is that I had flown overnight from the States before getting on the Isle of Man plane a couple of hours later. Consequently, I was more than a little jet-lagged!'

She knew just how unpleasant that could be, had often arrived abroad completely disorientated, half the time not even knowing where she was!

'I didn't know that,' she said quietly, her ice-cream finished now.

'Why should you? I— Here,' he reached out and gently ran his fingertip along the side of her mouth. 'Hey, it was only ice-cream,' he defended at her reaction.

Tory had jumped as if someone had hit her, at once feel-

ing the heated colour in her cheeks at her over-the-top reaction. 'Sorry,' she muttered awkwardly, wiping her mouth
with a tissue now. 'I—I wondered what you were doing.'

Jonathan raised dark brows. 'What did you think I was
doing?'

They had stopped walking now, were standing close together on the pavement, Tory not quite managing to meet
Jonathan's searching gaze.

What *had* she thought he was doing?

More to the point, why? Jonathan hadn't shown by so
much as a smile that he found her in the least attractive, so
why had her imagination jumped several steps ahead and
imagined he was about to kiss her a couple of minutes ago?

Which he obviously hadn't been!

She gave a bright, meaningless smile to cover up her
embarrassment. 'I guess I'm a little jumpy myself at the
moment,' she excused lightly, deliberately not answering
his question. 'If you're sure you feel up to it, I'm quite
happy to show you Douglas on the evening of Mad
Sunday.'

Jonathan looked serious. 'You're starting to make me
feel nervous now...'

Tory laughed at his worried expression. 'No, honestly,
you'll enjoy it,' she said with certainty. 'It's just a lot of
people having a lot of fun.'

Though she wasn't sure she was going to be one of them,
she decided later that afternoon, as she bathed and washed
her hair ready for going out that evening. The last time she
had been on the island for TT she had spent most of racing
week with Terry and his friends. Being in the company of
Jonathan McGuire was a different proposition completely!

What was he going to make of the bikers doing fantastic
wheelies up and down Douglas promenade, some of them
wearing only underpants to protect their modesty? The

pints and pints of beer being consumed by the crowds as they watched and cheered their antics? The impromptu parties? The bungee-jumping over the sea? The rock band playing on the quay?

If he had thought the drive around the TT course was 'interesting', then he was going to find this evening even more so!

'You look very nice, love,' her father told her as she joined them in the kitchen.

She must have changed her clothes half a dozen times before settling on the bright red tee shirt and black jeans, and she still wasn't sure she had chosen the right things to wear. Normally she would have gone to Douglas on her bike, and, like most of the revellers, she would have been in her biking leathers. But as Jonathan was driving them into Douglas...

He had thanked her very politely for taking him out when she'd returned him to the Byrnes' house earlier, had expressed pleasure in the drive back along the coast road—and promptly added, as he'd handed her the helmet back with obvious relief, that he didn't care if he never went on a motorbike again in his life—ever!

Tory had laughed, had still been smiling when she'd reached home a few minutes later—her father, as she had suspected, having very much enjoyed his war film in their absence!

'I'll do this, Mum,' she assured her mother now as she took over getting the Sunday tea: scones she had baked earlier that morning, fresh cream, and strawberry jam her mother had made a couple of months ago, also getting out a fruit cake her mother had made earlier in the week.

'Aren't you joining us, Tory?' her mother asked as Tory joined them with only a cup of tea in front of her. 'I hope you aren't dieting again, love,' she added worriedly. 'You really worried me the last time you did that.'

Rupert had decided a couple of years ago that she could do with losing a few pounds. Those 'few pounds' had resulted in even her size eights hanging loosely on her!

Her mother's answer to that, the next time Tory had gone home, had been to prepare all her favourite foods and make sure she ate them, ensuring that Tory was back to her original weight by the time she'd returned to London. Much to Rupert's annoyance!

'No, I'm not dieting, Mum,' she assured her wryly. 'Jonathan is taking me into Douglas this evening, and so—'

'Jonathan is?' her father echoed, brows raised speculatively.

Tory gave an inward sigh. Her parents, she knew, were no different from any others, and saw every man over twenty-five and under forty-five as a prospective son-in-law. She just wished that Jonathan McGuire didn't fit that particular criteria. Because he certainly wasn't suitable in any other way!

'Jonathan is,' she confirmed. 'So we'll probably pick up a snack to eat in Douglas somewhere.' There would be lots of places selling food this evening, from basic hotdogs to Chinese food.

'That'll be nice, love,' her father commented non-committally as he helped himself to the jam and cream to go with his scones.

She gave him a reproving look for his deliberate under-statement. 'It won't be nice at all,' she bit out impatiently. 'But without appearing rude to Madison, as well as her brother, I could hardly refuse his invitation!'

'Of course you couldn't, Tory,' her mother agreed. 'He seems a very pleasant young man?' she continued questioningly. Indeed, the flowers he had brought her earlier were now in pride of place in the sitting room.

Jonathan McGuire was not pleasant! A lot of other things, perhaps, but nothing as wishy-washy as pleasant!

'Any more war films on tonight, Dad?' Tory turned to him teasingly, unable to answer her mother.

'No.' His eyes twinkled at their shared joke concerning this afternoon. 'But there is a John Wayne film on later.'

Another of her father's favourites, she acknowledged unbegrudgingly. Her father, and her mother, worked extremely hard on the farm, especially this time of the year, and watching the television in the evenings was one of their avenues of entertainment.

Her cup of tea finished, Tory stood up abruptly. 'Jonathan was going to pick me up in about half an hour, but it's such a lovely sunny evening I think I'll walk over.' And she would avoid any more searching questions concerning Jonathan!

She picked up a black denim jacket in case it got cooler later that evening, hooking her thumb into it before throwing it over one shoulder.

'Have you got your key to get in? We'll probably be in bed when you get home,' her mother prompted.

'I'm not expecting to be that late,' Tory said firmly; she knew her parents liked to be in bed early, but a couple of hours in Douglas should be enough. More than enough when it was spent with Jonathan McGuire!

'Take your key just in case,' her father advised.

Tory had to admit that she felt a little disgruntled as she witnessed the knowing look that passed between her parents before she left the house. They were wasting their time if they imagined there was anything in the least romantic between Jonathan McGuire and herself; as far as Tory was concerned she was just being polite to the brother of a friend and neighbour!

'The lady doth protest too much, methinks...'

Where had that little taunting voice inside her come from? Wherever it was, she wished it would go straight back again!

Jonathan was good-looking, there was no doubting that. He was also extremely self-confident—but no longer arrogant? that little voice mocked again—much to Tory's increasing irritation! He had a certain charm, when he chose to exert it. He also hadn't been in the least concerned at admitting his aversion to the ride round the TT course earlier, so he wasn't pompously self-important, either.

There was also the way she had reacted to his touching her earlier, to remove the ice-cream from the side of her mouth...

She had made light of it at the time, but as it wasn't the first time it had happened—there had also been that tingling up her arm the previous day when they'd shaken hands—there was no doubting the fact that his merest touch sent little shock waves through her body.

But what did that mean?

She had been without a man in her life for too long; that was what it meant, she told herself sharply.

That was Rupert's fault again. His possessive attitude tended to frighten away any prospective boyfriends, in fact most people considered *he* was her boyfriend, to the point where she hadn't even been asked out by another man for over eighteen months.

No doubt Rupert, for all he hated the island, wouldn't have been agreeable to her coming here on her own either if he had thought there was the remotest possibility of her meeting any eligible men!

Oh, damn Rupert, she told herself crossly. He had had his chance a couple of years ago—and he had blown it!

She waved to the people camping in the neighbouring field as she strolled across to Jonathan's house; the island hotels and boarding houses simply couldn't accommodate a sudden influx of almost fifty thousand people, and a lot of visitors chose to bring tents and simply camp out. Tory's father had been letting them use the west field for as long as she could remember, laying on water and toilet facilities for them so that their stay could be as comfortable as possible, so much so that they usually had the same people come back to stay year after year.

The Byrne house looked mellowly welcoming in the early evening sunlight, the warmth of it's colours reflecting warmly.

It was only as Tory approached the front of the house that she became aware of the sound of music playing, the gentle strum of a guitar carried hauntingly in the still evening air.

Jonathan McGuire?

He had been less than forthcoming when she'd questioned him yesterday about the guitar, only finally grudgingly admitting that he played; if that was him playing now, then he played very well!

Tory made her way quietly round the side of the house, loath to disturb him when he wasn't even aware that anyone was listening; after all, he had said he would pick her up at seven o'clock—had no idea she would walk over instead.

He was sitting on the back balcony of the house, the guitar resting comfortably on his knee, long, artistic hands moving easily over the strings of the guitar as he played, the sound absolutely beautiful to the senses.

Tory hadn't really noticed his hands before, but now she

saw they were long and slender, brushing against the strings of the guitar almost in a loving caress.

She tried to place the tune, but it wasn't one she was familiar with. Nevertheless, it was poignantly beautiful, seeming to conjure up pictures in the mind of love found and then love lost, of heartbreak. To her surprise, Tory felt the sting of tears in her eyes...

It was—

'What the hell do you think you're doing, sneaking around, spying on me like this?'

That angrily rasping voice brought her back to a sudden awareness of her surroundings, blinking rapidly as she tried to clear the mesmerising beauty of the tune Jonathan had been playing from her brain.

Jonathan had stopped playing now, had risen indignantly to his feet, was glaring across the terrace at her with undisguised fury.

Oh, help!

CHAPTER FOUR

'I ASKED you what you're doing here.' His voice was icily cold.

Tory swallowed hard, sure she had never seen anyone this angry before. 'According to you, I was spying on you,' she finally said huskily. 'Except I wasn't spying on you at all. I decided to walk over. I—you were obviously—busy. I didn't like to disturb you,' she finished with a lame shrug.

Jonathan continued to look at her through narrowed grey eyes, obviously not too impressed with her explanation.

'You were right—you can play,' she said admiringly, giving a pained wince as his scowl only seemed to darken at these words.

But she was only telling the truth; he *could* play, quite beautifully, in fact.

'Have you ever thought of taking it up professionally?' she went on at his continued defensive silence. If he didn't say something soon—! Even his unmistakable anger was better than this coldly remote non-communication.

He gave her a flintily scathing glance before bending down to put his guitar away in the case, clicking the locks down decisively. 'And just what would you know about it?' he grated straightening to glare across at her dismissively.

She raised dark brows at his obvious scorn. Not only defensive, but back to being his rude self again. Oh, well, at least she knew where she stood with that!

'Absolutely nothing.' She confirmed what he wanted to

hear. 'But it sounded okay to me,' she added with sarcastic challenge.

His mouth twisted mockingly. 'Well, for your information, it was terrible. I take it you're ready to go into Douglas?' He eyed her casual clothes.

Obviously she was—but after his behaviour just now, she had the feeling he had changed his mind about taking her!

'If you are?' She gave a determined inclination of her head.

'Just give me a couple of minutes,' he rasped, picking up the guitar case and striding back into the house.

Take a seat. Would you like a drink while you're waiting? Obviously her unexpected arrival had robbed Jonathan of those manners he had said his mother taught him!

Tory sat down in the cane chair Jonathan had recently vacated, staring out across the fields stretching up towards the hills.

What was so awful about her having heard him play the guitar, for goodness' sake? She couldn't believe it was shyness on Jonathan's part; the man didn't have an un-self-confident bone in his arrogant body!

All she had done was take a stroll over here on a pleasant early-summer evening, but Jonathan had taken exception to having an unseen audience.

His mood hadn't improved in the slightest when he rejoined her on the terrace, also wearing black denims, but his tee shirt was black, too.

'You may need a jacket later,' Tory advised. 'The evenings can become quite cool.'

This good weather wasn't usually long-lasting on the Isle of Man. Situated in the Irish Sea, between England and Ireland, the island was also in the gulf stream, ensuring that they didn't have the really cold, icy weather England often did, but also meaning that in the summer months they rarely had temperatures that exceeded the mid-eighties. And it wasn't summer yet. In fact, TT Fortnight was known for its inclement weather!

Jonathan turned back into the house to collect a jacket, silent as they drove into Douglas, driving the Jaguar saloon car that belonged to the Byrnes as if he were actually in a race!

Tory sighed as they dropped down onto Douglas promenade, instantly caught up in a heavy flow of traffic. 'Perhaps this isn't such a good idea, after all,' she commented.

Jonathan gave her a brief glance. 'We'll be out of this jam in a few minutes,' he replied.

'I wasn't referring to this.' She waved a hand at the traffic and horse trams also travelling up and down in the middle of the road. 'You're still annoyed about earlier,' she continued at his enquiring look. 'I have no idea why, but it's clear you are.' She sighed again. 'And the evening of Mad Sunday in Douglas is for enjoying.'

Not tiptoeing around someone else's annoyance—especially when it seemed rather ridiculous to her!

'And you won't enjoy it with me in this mood,' Jonathan accepted grimly. 'I'm sorry, but you—you caught me in an unguarded moment earlier. Playing the guitar has only ever been for my own enjoyment before.'

She gave a half-smile. 'I don't think I've ever heard the tune before that you were playing; does it have any words?'

She knew by the way his eyes suddenly took on that flinty sheen that she had once again stepped on forbidden ground. Was there *any* subject that wasn't sensitive to this man?

His mouth thinned. 'If you thought my playing was bad, then you should hear me sing; tuneless doesn't even come into it!' He'd successfully avoided answering her question.

But she hadn't thought his playing was bad, and she had

said as much at the time. Besides, she didn't believe him
about the singing. And with good reason. He hadn't had
any music in front of him earlier, could obviously play a
tune by ear. And if he could do that, then she was sure he
wouldn't sing out of tune either.

'I think you're probably being modest,' she answered
him non-committally.

He turned to grin at her. 'I think you're humouring me,
Miss Buchanan!'

She relaxed slightly at this show of humour. 'I think I'm
trying to—Mr McGuire! Turn to the right up here,' she
advised quickly. 'We'll find somewhere to park in one of
the back streets.'

Easier said than done, they discovered during the next
ten minutes of looking, but finally managed to find a parking spot near the museum.

'The walk will do us good,' Tory said uncomplainingly
as they set off towards the noise of people enjoying themselves.

Jonathan took a light hold of her arm as they came out
onto the main street to be confronted by thousands of people milling about. 'If I lose you now, I'll never find my
way back to the car,' he offered by way of explanation as
she looked up at him questioningly.

'If we happen to lose each other, just remember we're
parked near the museum,' Tory hold him.

But still Jonathan kept that light hold, his hand warm
against the bare flesh of her upper arm. As it became more
and more crowded, the further they walked, Tory accepted
that the contact was necessary if they were not to get sep-
arated.

Even if it was doing strange things to her pulse-rate!
How could just the touch of his hand on her arm possibly

produce this heat inside her, make her legs feel slightly weak, too?

They stood and watched the bungee-jumping for a few minutes—a brief respite for Tory from the warmth of that hand!—laughing along with everyone else in the watching crowd when the second soul brave enough to try it ended up dunking her head in the sea below.

'I hope she hadn't just done her hair,' Tory said ruefully as the girl continued to bob up and down for several minutes.

'Have you ever tried that?' Jonathan asked as he looked up to where the cage for the start of the jump was situated. high above them.

Tory shook her head. 'I'm all for trying out new things— but I'm not stupid!'

Jonathan chuckled softly. 'I never for a moment thought you were.'

Just nosy and inquisitive!

Oh, well, Tory inwardly sighed; he was entitled to his opinion—even if it was wrong!

She turned to him. 'Have you ever tried English fish and chips?'

'Surely they would be Manx fish and chips?' he came back teasingly. 'And by chips I take it you mean fries?'

Tory had read a quote somewhere once, stating that England and America were two countries divided by a common language—and, from her own visits to the States, she was inclined to agree with that sentiment.

'You take it right.' She smiled. 'Although these chips are nothing like the thin fries you have in America. And the fish has batter on it. Probably not good for one's cholesterol levels, if you happen to be health-conscious.' She wrinkled her nose. 'But delicious to eat! Unfortunately, supposedly on the grounds of hygiene, they're no longer able to serve it in newspaper, but it still tastes good.'

'Lead me to it.' Jonathan took hold of her arm once again. 'After that huge lunch you gave me, I thought I was never going to feel hungry again, but I'm actually starving,' he realised. 'Must be all this sea air.'

'And I thought it was the bike ride this afternoon that had convinced you you would never feel hungry again!' She looked at him from beneath lowered lashes.

Jonathan shook his head at the memory. 'I've decided never to repeat the experience!'

Tory laughed huskily. 'You would probably feel differently if you had been the driver rather than the passenger.'

'Maybe.' But he didn't sound convinced. 'Is that live music I can hear?' He listened for a moment.

They were walking down the road beside the quay now, the crowd getting larger the further they walked. Tory could actually hear the rock band playing up on the temporary stage now, although she wasn't tall enough to see over the heads of the people in front of her. Jonathan, with his extra foot in height, seemed to be having no such trouble.

'They're good,' she offered after several minutes.

'This time I have to agree with you,' Jonathan drawled.

As opposed to her opinion earlier, concerning his guitar playing...!

She gave him a sceptical glance. 'We can get some food just along here.' She eased her way through the crowd until she got to the other side, waiting for Jonathan to join her before going inside the fish and chip shop.

No doubt this was going to be yet another culture shock for him, Tory decided as they joined the queue.

His life in Reno, involved in the running of casinos, must be so much more sophisticated. Although he had turned down the suggestion that he might like to see the island's casino while he was here...

'Is that compulsory?' Jonathan asked a few minutes later, the two of them back outside, watching Tory as she ate her food with her fingers.

She grinned up at him. 'Try it,' she invited laughingly; he had probably never eaten food with his fingers in his life before!

They were standing slightly on the edge of the listening crowd now; part of it, and yet somehow separate.

'If my family could see me now,' Jonathan muttered, before picking up a piece of the fish and putting it in his mouth.

That he liked what he was eating was obvious; there was a look of pure enjoyment on his face now as he began to eat the chips, too.

'Your mother is extremely beautiful,' Tory told him admiringly.

'She is,' he agreed. 'And Madison is very like her.'

Tory nodded. 'Then you must take after your father.' After all, Susan Delaney and Madison McGuire were both beautiful blondes.

'Probably,' Jonathan snapped, his expression once again as forbidding as the one he'd worn at the airport yesterday.

What had she said wrong now? Did Jonathan not get on with his father? Could that be the reason for this complete getaway to the Isle of Man?

'Which of your parents do *you* most resemble?' he demanded harshly.

Tory smiled; both her parents tended towards plumpness. What had once been her father's blond hair was now a wispy grey; her mother was also blonde, although, as she was only too happy to admit, it needed a little help from a bottle to be that colour nowadays.

'Neither of them,' she answered affectionately. 'I—'

'—joined by our very own Victory Canan!' the voice over the loudspeaker suddenly shouted.

Tory had been so engrossed in her conversation with Jonathan that she hadn't even realised the band had stopped playing, let alone that the MC had taken over the microphone.

'Victory!' the man called again, looking straight at her. 'Come and join us on the stage?' He held out a hand appealingly.

Tory didn't dare even glance at Jonathan as the crowd all turned to look at her too now, most with excited interest, some with obvious awe.

Neither was an emotion she particularly wanted at this moment!

'Victory Canan...?' Jonathan softly repeated at her side, eyes narrowed on her in cold assessment. 'You're *the* Victory Canan?'

The Victory Canan...

Somehow Jonathan managed to put a wealth of insult into those three words.

Yes...she was *the* Victory Canan! Jonathan had asked her earlier what she knew about music; the honest answer to that was...she knew a lot! Voted woman vocalist of the world for the third year running, with award after award given to her at a recent music awards ceremony, she would have had to be singularly stupid not to!

Even if Jonathan hadn't recognised her, he had definitely heard of her.

She moistened dry lips, at the same time tasting the food she had so recently enjoyed, which, as she looked up at Jonathan's harshly accusing expression, now lay heavily on her stomach.

Although she couldn't understand why!

Obviously he hadn't expected to be met by *the* Victory Canan when she'd come to taxi him to his sister's home, but that didn't alter the fact that he hadn't recognised her, either.

Or did he think she should have greeted him with the words, 'Hey, by the way, I'm actually Victory Canan, the singer. I suppose you've heard of me?'

For one thing, she wasn't that conceited, and for another, she came back to the island to enjoy the privacy that so many other well-known people could enjoy in peace on the Isle of Man! Here she could be completely herself, could walk down Strand Street, the main shopping street in Douglas, and merely have people say hello to her, or simply wish her well. She was one of those well-known people who could do her shopping locally and have absolutely no notice taken of her!

She put the rest of her uneaten fish and chips in a nearby bin before looking up at Jonathan once again. His gaze was steely, his jaw set coldly.

'You don't look much like your photographs!' he told her scathingly.

That wasn't surprising! Six years ago, when she'd first gone to London, she had developed an image for herself— an image that had adorned the front of newspapers inter-mittently for the last five years. An image she was becoming more and more glad to leave behind her when she came home...

Her mouth twisted wryly. 'There isn't a lot of call on the Isle of Man for coloured leathers, moussed hair, and streaks to match whatever colour clothes I happen to be wearing at the time!' Her make-up was much more dra-matic on stage, too; her face usually deliberately pale, with dark eye make-up, burgundy lipstick.

It was an image she left behind her when she came home.

In fact, she was surprised that the MC had recognised her; no one else seemed to have done until he'd called out her name.

But as she glanced back towards the stage she knew the answer to that particular puzzle, too; her cousin Terry was standing on the steps grinning at her, having spotted her in the crowd even if she hadn't seen him.

'Thanks!' she mouthed at him over the crowd, glaring her displeasure at his having revealed her presence.

She turned back to Jonathan, holding up her hands defensively. 'Look—'

'I take it Madison and Gideon know exactly who you are?' he said tautly.

She sighed. 'Yes, but—'

'I think your public wants you,' Jonathan cut in harshly as someone nearby began to clap, and the rest of the huge crowd quickly joined in.

'Jonathan—'

'You had better go,' he bit out coldly. The whistles and shouts were becoming louder by the second.

She gave him an impatient glare. 'I can explain—'

'There's nothing to explain—Victory,' he added scornfully—pointedly. 'And don't worry about me. I'm sure I can manage to find my own way back to the car! Near the museum, I think you said?'

In other words, he wasn't about to wait for her while she went up on stage to give the crowd the song they were asking for!

Her eyes flashed deeply blue. 'And just how am I supposed to get home?'

He looked about them at the warmly welcoming crowd, their faces alight with expectation. 'I'm sure one of your numerous fans will be only to happy to offer you a lift home! Terry, perhaps?' he suggested scathingly, obviously having seen the other man too now.

'Strange, I always thought it polite to leave with the person you arrived with.' Tory spat the words out angrily. 'Obviously we have different views on that!'

'Obviously,' he returned abruptly, his expression completely unbending. 'I'm sure you're very good at what you do, but I can't claim to have ever been a fan!' he finished insultingly.

The crowd had taken up a chant of her name now, the noise around them deafening.

'I had better not delay you any further then, had I?' she told him witheringly, before turning on her heel, her public smile on her face as she made her way up to the stage, much to the delight of the now cheering crowd.

'Do you know "Easy Street"?' she murmured to the group on stage, hoping they wouldn't mind this impromptu invasion of what was actually their show.

'Know it, love? We sing it.' The drummer smiled. 'But nowhere near as well as you do!'

She laughed her relief. 'Then let's do it!'

She became a complete professional as she launched into the song that had taken her to the top five years ago, knowing by the crowd's reaction that they were completely with her, singing and clapping along to the music.

All except one man...

Her last sight of Jonathan, after he'd given a last contemptuous glance in her direction, was as he turned on his heel and marched away, pushing his way through the rapidly growing crowd, as word of the presence of Victory Canan singing on stage spread like wildfire.

Well, damn him, she decided frustratedly.

Damn him to hell!

She wasn't going to apologise for who and what she was

to anyone, least of all the arrogant Jonathan McGuire. He could either take it or leave it.

He had chosen to leave it!

And her...

CHAPTER FIVE

'WHAT did you think you were doing, singing in some quayside concert in the middle of nowhere?'

Tory held the telephone receiver away from her ear, waiting for Rupert to stop shouting. Which he did—eventually.

'I thought,' she finally answered him in measured tones, determined not to lose her own temper, 'that I was exercising my own free will.'

Rupert might have set himself up as her keeper, but that was exactly what it was: a self-appointed role. And it wasn't one she was happy to let him take. Not any more.

'Some local reporter must have thought all his dreams had come true in one night. He sold the story and photographs of your impromptu concert the night before last to the daily newspapers over here,' Rupert continued in a disgruntled voice. '"Winner for Victory", "Impromptu Victory Concert", "A Home Win for Victory",' he quoted disgustedly.

Tory gave a wince at the terrible puns on her name. 'I thought you once told me any publicity was good publicity,' she reminded him dryly. 'Besides, all I did was sing a few songs.'

'According to the newspapers you were on stage for almost an hour and a half!' Rupert protested.

That was true. What had started out as singing one song to please the crowd had turned into a full-blown concert. The group had been more than pleased to back her as the audience shouted out for her to sing song after song. She had been amazed herself at the time that had elapsed when she'd finally managed to leave the stage.

Terry, for his sins, had been the one to drive her home later that night on the back of his bike, in apology for 'dropping her in it', he had admitted sheepishly.

Not that she had really minded. Except for the fact that Jonathan had walked off in disgust on learning she was Victory Canan in her professional life it had been a very enjoyable evening—the most fun she had had singing for years, she realised...

Jonathan's reaction to her professional persona was his own problem, she had decided as she lay in bed the night before, thinking about it. He could have no idea how refreshing it was not to be Victory Canan for even the few days of her visit here!

'Time passes quickly when you're having fun,' she told Rupert now.

'Did you get paid for it?' Rupert barked.

'Don't be ridiculous!' she snapped back, angry colour in her cheeks now, despite her earlier decision to remain calm. 'I was simply a member of the public asked to sing to a very appreciative audience.'

'Of course they were appreciative—you're Victory Canan, for goodness' sake!' Rupert was furious at the thought of her making an appearance on stage without consulting him first.

Victory Canan could ask thousands of pounds for a single performance, was worth millions in her own right from the sales of her records. Yes, she was Victory Canan, she acknowledged heavily.

Then she remembered her grinning, self-satisfied cousin, two nights ago, the couple of drinks she had shared with him and a few of his biker friends after the concert, and smiled herself now. 'Over here on the island I'm just Tory Buchanan.'

'Obviously,' Rupert retorted tightly. 'Every newspaper is questioning whether the ''soft flyaway hair'' and no make-up could possibly be a new image for you!'

Ah. Now they were getting to what was really bothering Rupert.

Her decision to leave London over a week ago had been made for two reasons: one she needed the rest and, two, she was tired of the rough, tough Victory Canan image! Rupert was more than aware of that.

'It isn't an image, Rupert,' she told him softly. 'It's the real me.' The real her that seemed, this last year or so, to have become buried under the pressure of being Victory Canan for almost fifty weeks of the year. Her bookings had sometimes seemed never-ending.

She had told Rupert before she left London that she wanted to change that image. Even the songs that she sang. Needless to say, Rupert had been absolutely horrified at the idea, and Tory knew exactly why that was.

Six years ago, raw and inexperienced, she had approached several agencies with the idea of asking them to manage her. Rupert, an Oxford graduate, new to the business himself, had been the only one willing to take the risk.

Looking back now, she could see he'd really had nothing to lose. If she were to be a success, then he would also bathe in that fame and glory, financially, of course. And it would benefit his agency to have a big star on its books. If she bombed he would lose nothing.

But she hadn't bombed. Had gone on from those first few performances Rupert had arranged for her to become a very marketable commodity. And now Rupert was very aware that changing her image, and performance, might make her less so...

'And who was the man, Tory?' Rupert curtly interrupted her musings.

'Man?' she echoed. 'What man?'

'"Miss Canan arrived at the concert with a tall, dark, mystery man".' Rupert was quoting from another of those newspapers. 'So who was he, Tory?' he repeated fiercely.

Her hand tightcncd about the telephone receiver. Someone had noticed that she'd arrived with Jonathan that night...?

Jonathan, if he saw any of those newspapers, was going to love this, she realised, and there was every possibility that he would, she acknowledged wearily; the island published a couple of its own newspapers, but the British dailies were delivered over here every day, too. In fact, the majority of the island's population had probably already received theirs, and so had seen the headlines about her concert and her 'mystery man'.

Not that the description didn't suit Jonathan perfectly. She had spent several hours in his company, and the little she did know about him had been dragged out of him!

'He's a friend of the family,' she told Rupert truthfully— if evasively!

'What sort of friend?' Rupert prompted shrewdly.

Until a couple of years ago Tory had made the mistake of being romantically involved with Rupert; it was a mistake she had paid for as, even after the personal relationship had fizzled out, Rupert seemed to think he had more than a professional claim on her.

'Male, obviously,' she returned impatiently.

'Oh, obviously,' Rupert echoed sarcastically. 'If there's a romance in the offing, Tory, then—'

'There isn't,' she snapped resentfully. 'I told you, he's a friend, nothing more.' After the other night, she wasn't even sure about that any more!

'The agency should handle all the publicity,' Rupert continued as if she hadn't interrupted him. 'You—'

'There isn't going to be any publicity!' Tory told him frustratedly. 'I—he's gone. Left the island,' she invented wildly.

Because if Rupert had picked up on that brief mention of a 'tall, dark, mystery man', then she was sure the world press would pick up on it, too—and try to follow up on it! She could just imagine Jonathan's horror—and fury!—if any of those reporters managed to track him down!

'He isn't a local, then?' The frown could be heard in Rupert's voice.

Her lips quivered wryly; she was well aware of Rupert's opinion of the island and its inhabitants. 'No, he isn't a local,' she confirmed.

There was a brief—and welcome!—silence on Rupert's end of the line. 'But even so—' he eventually began.

'Even so nothing,' Tory responded firmly. 'There's no story to write because there is no mystery man. Jonathan is—'

'Jonathan who?' Rupert instantly pounced.

Tory briefly wondered what his reaction would be if she were to tell him that Jonathan was actually the son of the legendary American actress Susan Delaney, and brother of Oscar-winning actress Madison McGuire. No doubt Rupert would come up with some lucrative publicity based on that information!

Which was precisely the reason he wasn't going to be given it!

'Just Jonathan, Rupert,' she replied levelly, wishing she hadn't even made that slight slip-up. 'Now, it's barely nine o'clock in the morning, Rupert, and I have things to do—as, I'm sure, do you.'

She had been up for hours, as it happened; life on a farm

this size began very early in the morning. With her mother incapacitated, a lot of the outside chores were left to Tory.

'Okay, Tory.' Rupert gave in irritably. 'But when are you coming home?'

Her mouth firmed. 'I am home.'

'You know what I meant,' he growled. 'Your mini-European tour begins in just under two weeks' time, and we still have a lot to—'

'I'm on holiday, Rupert—remember?' she jumped in. 'I'll think about the tour some time next week.' About Paris. And Amsterdam. And Berlin. And Zurich. And Rome. And all those nameless, characterless hotels she would have to stay in along the way!

'But—'

'Goodbye, Rupert,' she announced, before putting the receiver down.

She switched on the answer-machine. If, as Rupert had so angrily pointed out, the press were hot on the trail of a story, she did not intend to take any of their telephone calls.

Which left her with the problem of whether or not she ought to warn Jonathan of what was to come! He had left her in no doubt the other night as to exactly what he thought of her—and Victory Canan!—but that didn't alter the fact that if the world press started prowling about, as she suspected they might, then they would only have to add two and two together to realise that the 'tall, dark, mystery man' of the other night was actually Tory's tall, dark next-door neighbour!

As if in answer to her quandary the telephone began to ring next to her. The answer-machine went into action—to receive a message from the first of the overseas reporters to have tracked her down!

She had no choice; she would have to go and warn Jonathan!

It wasn't something she particularly relished doing. After the other night she could take a guess at what her reception was going to be, and what she had to tell Jonathan wasn't exactly going to endear her to him, either.

She turned as her father entered the house, having been up in the top fields the last couple of hours, checking on the sheep they had grazing there.

'Hello, love,' he greeted warmly, reaching under his arm to bring out the newspaper he had picked up on his drive home. 'You've made the front page again,' he told her happily, spreading the paper out on the kitchen table. '"A Home Win for Victory",' he read out with satisfaction.

Tory pulled a face. 'So I've already been told.'

'It's a good picture of you, too.' Her father hadn't looked up, so he hadn't noticed her less-than-pleased expression. 'For once it actually looks like the Tory your mother and I know and love!'

She couldn't resist strolling over to take a look, instantly understanding why Rupert was so angry about the picture in the newspapers.

'Sexy and sultry' were the words usually used to describe Victory Canan in her body-hugging leather clothes; the woman in this picture looked more like the girl next-door! She had obviously been enjoying herself when it was taken, laughing into the unseen camera, her hair having almost an ebony sheen to it, her eyes glowing, her cheeks flushed, a pale pink gloss on her lips. Anyone less like the sultry Victory Canan she couldn't imagine.

'Rupert isn't pleased,' she told her father distractedly, reading the article that went along with the picture.

Her father grimaced; the dislike was mutual between the two men. 'Been on the phone already, has he?' he asked knowingly.

'Hmm,' she confirmed vaguely, still reading the newspaper. Yes, there it was; 'Victory was accompanied by a tall, dark mystery man'!

She really didn't have a choice; she would have to go over and warn the 'mystery man'.

'Dad, I have to go out for a few minutes,' she told him awkwardly. 'If anyone rings—reporters, anyone like that—do *not* mention Jonathan's name. In fact, tell them I'm not here, either!' she added desperately as the telephone began to ring again.

'Ah.' Her father was still bent over the newspaper, having come to the part that mentioned her companion for the evening, too. He looked up, a sympathetic look on his face. 'How do you think Jonathan is going to react to that?'

'Well, considering he came to the island for peace, quiet and privacy—not very well!' she understated.

Her father chuckled. 'You had better get over there pretty smartish, then, hadn't you?'

Tory decided to go over on the bike. At least this time Jonathan wouldn't be able to accuse her of sneaking up on him; he simply couldn't miss the sound of the bike engine!

There was no sound of music from the back terrace this morning, so she went to the front door and rang the bell. And waited.

After almost five minutes of waiting, and despite the fact that the car was parked in the open garage, she decided Jonathan couldn't be at home, and turned to walk back to the bike. She would have to come back later. As long as no reporters had tracked her to the house by then. Otherwise she wouldn't be able to come back without leading the press to Jonathan's door. And he—

'Yes?'

She froze at the sound of that harshly challenging voice, turning slowly back towards the house.

Jonathan now stood in the open doorway, dark hair wet,

a dark blue robe pulled on over what appeared to be complete nakedness beneath, tanned legs bare beneath its knee-length hem, his feet also bare.

'I was taking a shower when I heard you arrive,' he told her. 'To what do I owe the honour of this visit?'

Tory didn't need to be told he was still angry at the public way he had found out she was actually Victory Canan; his mocking expression as he looked her up and down in the black leathers said it all for him.

'The honour is all mine,' she returned dryly, instantly stung into being defensive. 'I—could I talk to you for a few minutes?'

'I thought you already were,' he drawled.

'Privately,' she said firmly.

He looked about them. Apart from her parents' farm and a couple of hundred sheep, uninhabited countryside surrounded them, and his gaze was scornful as it returned to her. 'I don't think the sheep are going to pose any problem to that, do you?' He didn't even try to disguise his sarcasm.

Tory drew in a deep breath, her hand tightening about the strap of the crash helmet she carried. She sighed. 'You could try offering me a cup of coffee,' she felt stung into reproving.

'Is what you have to say going to take long enough for that?'

Her cheeks coloured resentfully. She hadn't had to come here today, could have just left him to the vultures. At least that way she wouldn't have had to put up with his rudeness—again!

He stepped back, opening the door wider. 'Would you like to come in for coffee—Victory?' he mocked.

'Thank you,' she accepted stiffly, marching past him into the house and going straight to the kitchen at the back, having sat there with Madison dozens of times drinking coffee as the two of them cooed over baby Keilly. There would certainly be no such cooing today!

She tried not to watch Jonathan as he moved about the kitchen getting the coffee ready. It wasn't that she had never seen a man dressed only in a robe before, it was just that this man happened to be Jonathan McGuire!

He looked somehow younger with his hair still damp and inclined to curl, and what she could see of his chest seemed as tanned as his bare legs and feet. Perhaps he didn't spend all his life in the false brightness of casinos!

He stopped what he was doing for a moment, looking across at her with assessing eyes. 'I suppose there must be thousands of people—make that millions!—who would be only too happy to be making coffee for Victory Canan,' he commented.

But not him, Tory acknowledged inwardly. Jonathan looked as if he would rather be doing anything else but making her coffee—preferably strangling her!

'Make that millions of *men*,' he corrected.

Tory shot him a narrow-eyed glare. 'I do have female fans, too!'

'Really?' He raised sceptical dark brows. 'I can't think why.'

Her cheeks flushed fiery red as she desperately tried to hang on to her temper—it really wouldn't help anything if they ended up in a slanging match! 'Possibly because I actually can sing. I'm also a polished performer,' she defended resentfully.

'Really?' he came back again. 'I wouldn't know. As I told you; I've never been a fan.'

He wasn't about to make this easy for her, was he? Okay, so he felt he had been duped, made a fool of, but that was only his version of what had happened. Hers was completely different; there had been no deliberate act to deceive

on her part; she was simply Tory Buchanan, Dan and
Thelma Buchanan's daughter, when she came back to the
island.

'Thanks.' She accepted the mug of coffee he put in front
of her.

'I suppose, considering who you are, it really should be
in bone china cups, but—'

'Will you just stop this, Jonathan?' she cut in wearily,
eyes flashing deeply blue. 'You've been to the farm; you
know it isn't like that. Hey, I even cooked lunch for you
on Sunday!'

His mouth tightened as he sat opposite her at the kitchen
table. 'Amazing,' he drawled, making no effort to disguise
his sarcasm.

Tory took a sip of the black, unsweetened coffee before
answering—at the moment she felt more in need of raw
caffeine than putting Jonathan McGuire in his place!

'It's a sight more than you've done for me,' she eventually exclaimed.

'True,' he replied thoughtfully. 'How did the concert go
the other night?' He changed the subject mildly.

Tory shot him another resentful glare, knowing he wasn't
really interested. If he had been then he wouldn't have left
the way he had!

'See for yourself,' she declared, pulling the front page
of her father's newspaper from the back pocket of her leathers to throw it down on the table in front of Jonathan; her
father had been only to happy to loan it to her in the circumstances!

Jonathan's expression, as he read the article accompanying Tory's photograph, slowly changed from disdain to
frowning concentration, to scowling anger!

Tory waited for that anger to reach verbal proportions.

Jonathan stood up abruptly, taking the newspaper with

him as he read the article a second time. 'Wonderful!' he finally looked up from the page to rasp angrily. 'Just wonderful!' He flung the newspaper back down onto the table, hands clenched furiously at his sides.

Tory swallowed hard. 'I—'

'Not one word, Victory,' he bit out tautly. 'Not one damned, single word—or I'm likely to strangle you first and think about the consequences afterwards!'

That was what she had thought earlier—but he looked as if he were more than capable of doing exactly that now!

Anyone would think she had done this on purpose! Whereas in actual fact she was no more thrilled at having her privacy invaded in this way than he was.

Although that chilling glitter to the narrowed grey eyes, the thin, angry line of his mouth, angrily clenched jaw, didn't give the indication he was in the least concerned at how *she* felt!

'I—'

'I said, not a word, Victory,' he reminded her through gritted teeth.

' "I" isn't a word. It's a—'

'Don't say I didn't warn you, Victory. Twice!' Jonathan muttered, even as he pulled her roughly to her feet.

And straight into his arms. Knocking the breath from her body. Not that she would have been able to breathe anyway, when his mouth had just savagely taken possession of hers...!

She was being kissed by Jonathan McGuire!

Thoroughly.

Completely.

Contemptuously...!

Tory wrenched her mouth free of his. Not an easy feat when she was held so tightly in his arms she could feel every muscle and sinew of his body pressed firmly against hers.

'Stop it.' She pushed ineffectually at the steel bands about her that were Jonathan's arms. 'Jonathan—'

'I have no intention of stopping anything, Victory—'

'My name is Tory!' she protested, still pushing at his arms.

Those steel bands tightened even more. 'You're Victory Canan,' he grated. 'I still can't believe I didn't recognise you!' He shook his head in self-disgust as he looked down at her. 'I've been reading about your exploits in the newspapers for years. The wild parties. The men. The—'

'Doesn't the half-truth in that newspaper—' she gestured towards the kitchen table, where he had thrown the newspaper down in his anger '—indicate how much credence you should give those other stories?'

Yes, there had been parties—it was part of her image to be seen at parties with the rich and famous. Yes, there had been men—but not in the way Jonathan was implying; she simply didn't have time the way her life was now to give to a relationship. Rupert had been her last serious involvement, and in the last two years there had simply been a succession of male escorts to take her to parties, to be seen with—nothing else.

It was that very image he was talking about that she wanted to rid herself of...!

Although she could see by Jonathan's savage expression that he didn't want to hear any of that, that he wouldn't believe her if she told him how lonely it was at the top.

She wouldn't have believed it herself six years ago, when she had gone off to London in search of fame and success—a bit like Dick Whittington, who had believed the streets of London were paved with gold! Well, they were, if you had the talent—and luck—to succeed, but she had

had no idea of the personal price she would have to pay for such success.

To Rupert, as she had eventually learnt to her emotional cost, she was just a vehicle for his own success.

To other men—those that dared to approach her, that was—she was a trophy to wear on their arm for a while. The real Tory was of no interest to them whatsoever.

But Jonathan, furiously angry Jonathan, who believed he had been taken for a fool, wasn't in any sort of mood to listen to that!

He stared at her contemptuously. 'If only half those stories are true…!'

On the surface, all of them were true. But in actual fact none of them were. Because none of them told the story of her isolation, her loneliness, of how night after night—when she wasn't away somewhere performing!—she went home alone to her sumptuous apartment, having long passed the stage of relishing her privacy, now only feeling her solitude, the silence that simply went on and on, hour after hour, night after night.

Only here, back on the island, with her parents, could she find contentment of spirit as well as a release from that exhausting loneliness.

She sighed heavily, giving a weary shrug. 'Perhaps it's true what they say; people will only believe what they want to believe.'

Jonathan's face darkened. 'Are you accusing me of being prejudiced where you're concerned?' he said sternly.

She gave a humourless smile. 'I'm accusing you of treating me like every other person does—except my parents, family and my island friends—and that's as nothing more than a money-spinning sex symbol!' She spat the last words out disgustedly.

He looked down at her with knowing eyes. 'Poor little rich girl, is that it?'

She flinched at his unmistakable scorn. 'You have no idea,' she replied.

'Tell me about it,' he encouraged.

She was still held in his arms, still pressed against the lean length of his body; she was having trouble thinking straight at all! Let alone making sense of it all.

When she was younger, before she'd gone to London, like all teenagers she had read magazine articles about how the rich and famous bemoaned the loneliness they had found along with their success, quoting that old cliché that money couldn't buy you happiness—and she had believed they were all talking a lot of nonsense. Except it wasn't. She had been lonelier for real friendship in the last six years than she ever had before.

Jonathan watched her with narrowed eyes as the emotions flickered and flittered across her face, looking more puzzled now than angry.

Tory looked up at him from beneath lowered lashes, tears poised on the edge of those lashes. For some reason this man's opinion mattered to her—and at the moment he felt only contempt for her.

Jonathan suddenly put her away from him and looked down at her with flinty grey eyes. 'Tell me,' he said, 'does this act usually work?'

Tory blinked, taken aback by this sudden—and unwarranted!—renewal of attack. 'I don't know what you mean...'

'Sure you do,' Jonathan attacked, hands thrust deeply into the pockets of his robe. 'And, you know, for a few moments there it almost worked. I was actually starting to feel sorry for you. But for the tears, I just might have believed you. They were a little over the top, I'm afraid.'

Tory blinked back the offending tears once again. Act? Act…! How dared he? Just who did he think he was?

'Indeed?' Her voice shook with anger now, and she bent down to grab her helmet up from where she had put it on the kitchen floor earlier.

Jonathan nodded. 'Where women are concerned, they usually come into play when all else fails.'

Her eyes flashed deeply blue. 'Then I won't bore you with my act any longer!'

'Oh, I'm not bored, Victory,' he assured her. 'In fact, for a few moments I was completely entertained.'

Tory had no wish to know which few moments he was referring to. 'Nevertheless, it's time I was going,' she told him frostily. 'I hope you enjoy the rest of your stay, Mr McGuire,' she added insincerely, turning to march out of the kitchen, her head high.

Arrogant, insulting…!

She had come over here today out of a sense of obligation, had felt she at least owed it to Jonathan to let him know of the repercussions he might encounter from Sunday evening.

Now, as far as she was concerned, he could take care of himself!

She was sure it was something he was good at!

CHAPTER SIX

'I THINK you should hear this one, love.' Tory's father, in the process of listening to the messages that had been left on the answer-machine throughout the day, turned to speak to her as she entered the kitchen.

Tory looked over at him with dull, lifeless eyes. Her anger towards Jonathan McGuire had stayed with her on the drive home, and through most of the afternoon. Now it was early evening and she was feeling decidedly deflated.

Jonathan had been rude the day she'd met him at the airport, and intermittently so since then, but she believed he had been deliberately hurtful this morning.

Why? That was what was puzzling her now.

He had wanted to believe the worst of her, seemed to enjoy insulting her and mocking what he had hinted were her crocodile tears.

Again, she asked herself, why?

'Okay, Dad,' she agreed wearily as she sat down at the kitchen table to listen.

Although she couldn't imagine what was going to be so different about this call; most of the daily newspapers had already phoned her, and without exception they had all wanted to know more about the mystery man who had accompanied her on Sunday evening. Curiosity she had no intention of satisfying!

'Tory? Jonathan—Jonathan McGuire.' The message began to play back, causing Tory to sit up straighter in her seat, her expression wary now as she looked across at her father; his brows were raised ruefully.

She couldn't imagine why; if Jonathan had called just to insult her some more, her father had already heard it once!

There was really no need for Jonathan to have added 'McGuire'; contrary to what he might think of her, she knew no other Jonathans. Besides, that attractive American drawl was unmistakable!

'—owe you an apology,' Jonathan continued tersely. 'I—could you call me once you've received this message?' The call ended with an abrupt click of the receiver.

Could she—?

The man had some nerve calling her at all, after the things he had said to her this morning, let alone expecting her to return the call!

'Tory...?'

She looked across at her father, knew by the slightly reproving look on his face that she was about to hear a gentle lecture on forgiving and forgetting. As in earlier years, the look was enough.

She sighed. 'Dad, if you could have heard the things he said to me this morning—'

'I think I might have been a bit annoyed myself if I were in his shoes,' her father cut in softly. 'Let's face it, Tory. With a famous mother, sister and brother-in-law, the poor man has probably had enough media intrusion in his life already, without encountering it here, of all places.'

He was right. She knew he was right. But—

'He just wants to apologise, love.' Her father once again cut in on her mutinous thoughts, smiling encouragingly. 'I don't suppose it's something he does too often,' he added, obviously having summed the younger man up during lunch on Sunday.

Tory continued to look mutinous for several seconds. And then she began to smile; she never had been able to resist her father's unfailing good humour. 'It might be worth listening to that,' she conceded with a smile.

'You'll call him back, then?' her father encouraged.

'I'll think about it,' she compromised, not sure she could listen to what she was sure would be merely a lip-service apology on Jonathan's part; he probably just didn't want to upset his sister's nearest neighbours!

'That's my girl.' Her father ruffled her hair affectionately on his way to the door. 'Your mother is resting her ankle before tea, and I'm just going outside to check on the chickens before settling down for the evening.'

In other words, she had about ten minutes' uninterrupted privacy in which to return Jonathan's call. Tory acknowledged her father's ploy ruefully.

The thing was, she didn't want to return his call, had no wish to listen to an insincere apology on Jonathan's part and an even less sincere acceptance on her own part; Jonathan had made his opinion of her more than clear this morning.

She paced up and down the kitchen, all the time aware of the precious minutes ticking away.

Oh, damn him, she finally decided impatiently. She would listen to his apology, accept it, and that would be an end to it. Then everyone, including her parents, would be happy.

'Jonathan McGuire,' he answered her call tersely.

Her hand tightened about the phone, antagonism welling up inside her. 'Victory Canan,' she came back challengingly, very aware that he had chosen to call her 'Tory' on the message he'd left on the answer-machine earlier.

'Tory.' His voice softened in recognition. 'You received my message?'

'Obviously,' she snapped.

'Otherwise you wouldn't be calling at all,' he acknowledged dryly.

'No,' she returned curtly.

Jonathan chuckled softly. 'You're still annoyed with me?'

'Yes,' she confirmed abruptly.

'And with good reason,' he conceded with a sigh. 'I owe you an apology—'

'Accepted,' she bit out. 'Was that all?'

'No, it damn well was not all!' he came back furiously. 'I would like to invite you out to dinner.'

Tory became very still, frowning her puzzlement. He wanted to invite her out to dinner...?

'Well, not out exactly,' he went on, almost as if he had heard her thoughts. 'After the way you were recognised on Sunday I'm not sure that would be a good idea. I wondered if you would like to come over here for dinner?'

Over there? But—

Tory was aware she was reacting like a gauche schoolgirl being invited out by the handsomest boy in the school— even worse, she was behaving as if she had never been invited out by a man before!

'Have you forgotten about the media interest in us?' she reminded him. Her father had already dealt very effectively with a couple of reporters who had turned up at the farm. But they were still lurking about at the end of the long driveway to the house.

'No, I haven't forgotten.' Jonathan's voice had hardened. 'But I'm sure from previous experience you must be more than capable of getting past that.'

Getting by nosy reporters, he meant, Tory accepted irritably. And that might be true. She just wasn't sure she wanted to go to all that trouble on Jonathan McGuire's behalf...

'Can you think of one good reason why I should accept your invitation?' she questioned scathingly.

'Because I asked nicely?' he came back.

Yes, he had certainly done that. He had also apologised for his insulting behaviour earlier. Yet Tory still questioned his motives...

'Can you actually cook?' she said slowly. 'Or is this just a ruse to have someone cook dinner for you?'

Jonathan laughed throatily. 'Why don't you come over here and find out?'

Because she wasn't sure she wanted to spend the evening with him! He hadn't only insulted her earlier—he had kissed her, too.

And for a few seconds she had responded...!

She would be lying to herself if she said she didn't find Jonathan attractive. But it was an attraction that was going nowhere. She had already wasted three years of her life— and her love—on Rupert; falling for Jonathan would be even more of a disaster.

'You're taking an awful long time to make your decision,' Jonathan finally drawled. 'Don't tell me you're scared, Tory?'

'Of you?' Her tone was scornful as she bristled defensively.

'Of my cooking,' he came back mockingly.

He hadn't meant any such thing! But, no, she wasn't scared. Not of him. Or anything else, for that matter.

'What time would you like me to come over?' she prompted stiffly.

'Seven-thirty for eight?'

'Fine,' she accepted briskly. 'I'll see you then.' She rang off before he could make any more mocking remarks.

She had been managed, bulldozed, railroaded!

Into spending the evening with Jonathan...

*   *   *

'You look nice, love.' Her mother, her bandaged ankle resting on top of a stool, raised her head from reading the newspaper, looking over the top of her glasses as Tory entered the room.

Her mother's praise for her appearance was more than welcome. Tory didn't know what it was about Jonathan, but she always had trouble deciding what to wear when she knew she was seeing him!

It wasn't that she didn't have clothes for most occasions; she had a wardrobe full of them. She was just never sure what the occasion actually was when she was meeting Jonathan!

If she had been having dinner with any other man, in other circumstances, then there wouldn't have been a problem, either. But Jonathan already seemed to have the idea that Victory Canan was a siren in leathers, and Tory Buchanan was a jean-clad biker.

Which was why tonight she was wearing a fitted plain dark blue dress—which matched her eyes—sleeveless, knee-length. Her legs were silky in flesh-coloured tights, and two-inch heels on her shoes gave her some height. Her hair was newly washed, falling silkily down onto the shoulders, her make-up light, just blusher highlighting her cheekbones. Her lip-gloss was her only defiant gesture—it was bright cherry-red, giving her mouth a sexily pouting look.

Take that, Jonathan McGuire, she had told her reflection in her wardrobe mirror a few minutes ago; tonight she was neither the Tory Buchanan that Jonathan had come to know, nor the Victory Canan that he didn't want to know!

'Thanks, Mum.' She smiled gratefully at her mother for her confidence-boost. 'Is Dad ready?' she prompted lightly.

'He's strolled outside to chat to the reporters at the end of the driveway, at the same time letting slip into the conversation that he's popping out on his weekly visit to your grandmother's in a few minutes.' Her mother grinned. 'So if you sneak out the side door while he's distracting them, and get into the back of the car, he'll be with you shortly.'

It was ridiculous that they had to go to such subterfuge just so that Tory could go out for the evening. But more reporters had started arriving at the farm in the last hour—keeping a discreet distance at the end of the driveway, but watching every move at the farmhouse nonetheless.

'I'll see you later, then.' She moved to kiss her mother warmly on the cheek.

'Just give your Dad a call when you're ready to come home.' Her mother nodded.

If Jonathan carried on his insulting behaviour of this morning, that shouldn't be too long!

Hiding in the back of the car, a blanket pulled over the top of her head, wasn't the most elegant way to depart for an evening out. But without it, Tory knew from experience, she wouldn't be able to get out at all.

'You can come out now,' her father told her with amusement a few minutes later.

Tory sat up on the back seat, brushing her ruffled hair back into some sort of order as her father turned the car down the drive to the Byrnes' house.

In other circumstances she could have walked over, as she had on Sunday evening. But it was that over-confidence on Sunday that had now made it impossible.

'Have fun,' her father said lightly once he had parked the car in front of the house.

'Give my love to Nan,' Tory replied distractedly, and watched as he drove away, somehow reluctant to approach the front door.

Jonathan's moods were mercurial, to say the least—and she had no idea which one he was going to be in this evening!

'Tory!' he greeted her warmly, seconds after she had rung the doorbell, the speed with which he had answered taking her completely by surprise—it meant he must have been waiting in the hallway for her arrival! 'How did you get here?' he looked out at the deserted driveway.

She looked up at him with wary blue eyes, those insults he had flung at her earlier still very much in her mind. 'My father drove me over. I'll call him when I want to leave,' she informed him pointedly.

Jonathan grinned as he easily picked up on her warning that she might want to leave in the next few minutes if he was as insulting as he had been this morning. 'You're looking very lovely this evening,' he told her huskily.

'Thank you.' Her wariness didn't lessen one iota at his compliment. 'So are you,' she returned archly.

And he was. His grey silk shirt emphasised the muscled width of his shoulders and narrowness of his waist, and was matched with fitted black denims.

He quirked dark brows. 'Pleasantries over, would you like to come inside? Or do you expect me to serve your dinner out here?' he asked mockingly.

'It's such a pleasant evening,' she replied, as she preceded him into the house, 'that it might be rather nice to eat outside.'

'I agree with you.' Jonathan nodded. 'That's why I've set the table out on the terrace.' He walked straight through the sitting room and out of the French doors at the far end.

Tory, following behind him, felt her stomach do a somersault before settling back in place as she took in the romantic setting.

The cane table had been set with cut glass and silver cutlery; a silver candelabra with green candles stood at its centre. Two cane chairs stood almost side by side as they looked out over the garden and distant hills.

She turned to give Jonathan a searching look from beneath lowered dark lashes. The scene was set for seduction...

Jonathan returned her gaze unblinkingly. 'As you said, it's too beautiful a night to sit inside,' he agreed lightly. 'Now, can I get you red or white wine?'

'That depends on what we're eating.' There was no way, when the atmosphere seemed so charged with expectation, that she wanted to mix her drinks, even red and white wine. Ending up more than a little drunk could just convince this man that all her bad publicity was true, after all. If he didn't already believe that...

'Fish to start, steak for main course, so it's your choice.' He shrugged.

'Red, then, please,' she accepted, moving to sit down on the swinging seat, reluctant to actually sit down and embrace the intimacy of that table set for two.

It had been a mistake to come here, she told herself once Jonathan had gone back into the house to get the wine. She didn't know what she had expected when she accepted Jonathan's invitation, but it certainly wasn't this!

Scared, Tory? She asked herself that now. For years she had been regretting the fact that she couldn't have dates and meet men in the way that other women could, and now that she had met one, been invited to dinner by him, she was so nervous her hand was shaking slightly as she reached out to take the glass of red wine Jonathan now held out to her.

'Hmm, Gevrey-Chambertin,' she murmured appreciatively after her first sip. 'Oh, don't look so worried, Jonathan.' She chuckled at his stunned expression. 'I'm not such a wino I can guess a wine just from its taste; I just happen to know that Gideon keeps this particular one in the cellar!'

He sat down on the swing-seat next to her, long legs stretched out in front of him, whereas Tory's feet, even in shoes with two-inch heels, hardly reached the floor!

He turned to look at her. 'Do you see a lot of Maddie and Gideon when they're on the island?' he said slowly.

'If I'm at home, too, yes,' she responded, very conscious of the fact that his arm was stretched along the back of the seat behind her. Not touching her. But she could feel his warmth, anyway.

Jonathan shook his head. 'They've never mentioned knowing you,' he murmured.

She laughed dismissively. 'That isn't surprising; I don't go around telling people that I know them, either!'

Jonathan gave the ghost of an answering smile before turning to look out at the distant hills. 'What do you think of Gideon?'

Tory was taken aback by the question. Gideon was this man's brother-in-law, for goodness' sake; what did he expect her to say in answer to a question like that?

'I think he's a wonderful husband and father,' she answered guardedly.

'I know that part,' Jonathan dismissed impatiently. 'What do you think of him as a man?'

Her frown deepened and she stiffened resentfully. 'Exactly what are you implying...?' After the insults Jonathan had levelled at her earlier today, she didn't like the turn this conversation had taken at all!

'Implying—?' he repeated. 'I'm not implying anything like that, Tory,' he answered impatiently as he picked up on the reason for her indignation. 'I know for a fact that Gideon is head over heels in love with my sister.'

'Then—?'

Jonathan stood up. 'Forget I asked,' he rasped, putting his own barely touched glass of wine down on the table.

'I'll just go and get our first course,' he grated, before striding back to the kitchen.

Tory was more puzzled than ever. Obviously she knew Gideon and Madison, but it was Madison she knew best—Gideon tended to be rather a remote figure. Except when it came to his daughter, Tory remembered with affection. He was a man obviously deeply in love with his wife, but who liked to keep his emotions to himself—except when it came to his baby daughter: he was like putty in Keilly's little hands!

But somehow Tory didn't think that was what Jonathan had wanted to know...

'Here we are.' He arrived back with plates of smoked salmon, placing them on the table before lighting the candles; there was barely a breeze to disturb their flame. 'Would you like some white wine with this, or are you going to stick to the red?'

'Stick with the red. Thank you.' She was still a little disturbed by their earlier conversation. 'Don't you approve of Gideon?' she probed once they were seated at the dining table, having tasted the smoked salmon and found it to be deliciously fresh.

'I told you, I have no doubts of his devotion to Maddie and the baby,' Jonathan answered stiffly. 'His father was John Byrne, you know,' he added abruptly.

As it happened, yes, she did know. She also knew that the legendary actor had died over thirty years ago in a car crash. While drunk. Having apparently left his wife and young son for another woman several months earlier.

'Gideon isn't responsible for who or what his father was,' she said gently.

Jonathan gave her a narrow-eyed look, barely touching his own food. 'You don't believe that we are the genes we inherit from our parents?'

'If you're asking whether I believe Gideon is going to turn into a drunk and adulterer, because that's what his father was, then no, I don't believe it,' Tory answered firmly, shaking her head. 'Things like social background, education, one's own personality strengths and weaknesses have to be taken into account, too. After all, we don't grow up as clones of our parents. No two children in a family, unless they are identical twins, are ever exactly the same. And even twins have different personalities.'

'Perhaps it's easy for you to dismiss. You obviously know who you are,' Jonathan responded harshly, not missing her questioning look.

She laughed softly; this conversation had become altogether too heavy for comfort. 'Do any of us know that? Do any of us really want to know that?' She was deliberately flippant in an effort to lighten the atmosphere between them.

Jonathan sighed. 'That's what I'm here to find out.'

Her eyes widened. 'Who you are...?'

He nodded. 'Amongst other things.'

'You're Jonathan McGuire,' she told him teasingly.

He returned her gaze steadily. 'Am I?'

Tory shrugged. 'That's who you said you were.'

'Then that's who I must be.' He gave an inclination of his head.

Tory raised dark brows. 'Aren't you a little young for a mid-life crisis?'

Wasn't she a little young for that herself? And yet she knew she was going through a similar soul-searching period herself...

He drew in a harshly ragged breath, his smile, when it came, seeming somewhat forced. 'You're right. I am.' He relaxed slightly, eyeing the barely touched food on her plate. 'Eat up, or it will get cold.'

'It's already cold,' she said.

'Just testing,' he came back teasingly. 'And you were right about the wine; I had to raid Gideon's wine cellar earlier, when I realised I had forgotten to buy any.'

'I'm sure he won't mind.' She smiled.

The earlier tension seemed to have abated now. Although Tory wasn't absolutely sure of why it had been there in the first place. Jonathan obviously liked his brother-in-law, approved of him as a husband for his younger sister. And yet...

Jonathan was turning out to be as enigmatic as she knew Gideon to be. In fact, if she hadn't been told Jonathan was Madison's brother, it would have been all too easy to assume he was Gideon's. The two men weren't only alike in temperament, they looked alike, too—both tall and dark, with those grey eyes that revealed so little of their inner thoughts.

Jonathan stood up suddenly. 'I'll just go and check on the steaks.'

'Can I do anything to help?' she instantly offered.

'Did I do anything on Sunday?' he taunted.

She gave that some thought. 'You ate my food without complaint,' she finally remembered.

'For a superstar, you aren't a bad cook!' came his satirical parting shot, before he disappeared inside the house carrying their empty plates.

For a bigoted idiot, neither was he, she discovered a few minutes later when she bit into her first mouthful of steak. The meat had been marinated in something—honey and mustard she could discern, but the rest of it was a mystery to her. It was the most delicious steak Tory had ever eaten!

'This is very good,' she told Jonathan with feeling.

She hadn't been sure she would be able to eat this evening at all, let alone feel like stabbing with her fork the first person who tried to take this steak away from her!

Jonathan grinned at her obvious appreciation. 'Am I forgiven for my rudeness this morning now?' he prompted huskily. 'I was angry—very much so,' he conceded grimly. 'But I really shouldn't have taken that anger out on you in the way that I did. You, and your family, have been extremely kind to me since I arrived here.'

She took another sip of the fruity red wine before answering, aware that he was obviously sincere in his apology. Though some of the things he had accused her of this morning were actually unforgivable. But perhaps—with the last five years of speculative publicity behind her—understandable? that little voice inside her head reasoned.

Maybe, she accepted grudgingly.

'Can I take a raincheck on answering that until after we've had dessert?' she came back lightly.

He gave a rueful smile. 'That depends on how much you like strawberries and cream.' He grimaced.

She gave an impish grin. 'Love them!'

Jonathan gave an inclination of his dark head. 'In that case, I'm happy to wait.'

The evening stayed dry and warm, the flickering candles in the centre of the table their only illumination as it grew dark.

They talked of everything and nothing. Mainly nothing, Tory realised as they lingered at the table after finishing their meal, to drink glasses of port. She was reluctant to talk about her highly charged career, and Jonathan seemed reluctant to talk about anything other than the island and the few places he had managed to see so far on his visit here.

Pretty innocuous stuff, Tory inwardly surmised. But at

least they weren't arguing or, even worse, insulting each other.

She was feeling more than a little mellow from the wine and port she had drunk. Jonathan appeared even more attractive than usual to her glowing gaze, as she admired the strength in the squareness of his jaw, his mouth, which was looking extremely kissable, and as for those eyes—!

Had she really thought they were flinty and cold the first time she saw him? Now they only appeared warmly caressing as he looked at her over the top of his glass, glittering almost silver in the candlelight as his eyes lingered on the fullness of her lips.

'Tory…?' he questioned slowly, even as he put his port glass down on the table.

She swallowed hard. Jonathan was going to kiss her. Again. And she wanted him to!

She moved slightly to accommodate that kiss as his head bent down to hers, her heart seeming to leap behind her breasts as he sipped and tasted at her lips, not touching her in any other way, but seeming to hold her captive anyway.

'You really are a very beautiful woman.' The warmth of his breath stirred the dark tendrils of hair at her temple as he spoke.

And he was a gorgeous man! Everything that tall, dark, and handsome should be. Although she wasn't about to let him know that…!

'Thank you,' she accepted huskily.

'Tell me…' He looked down at her searchingly, one of his hands moving to smooth the hair back from her brow. 'Are you involved with anyone at the moment?'

'Involved with anyone?' she repeated tautly.

He nodded. 'That guy Terry. Or possibly someone else.'

Tory stiffened defensively. '"That guy Terry" happened to be my cousin. The brother of Saturday's bride. Do you think I would be here with you, like this if I were involved with someone else?'

He smiled gently, grey gaze warm on her flushed cheeks. 'I wasn't trying to be insulting, Tory.'

Of course he wasn't, she accepted impatiently; he really didn't have to try! But because she still felt so defensive around this man, it was all too easy for her to feel insulted...

'I'm sorry.' She grimaced.

Jonathan shook his head. 'Your reserve is understandable, Tory,' he conceded. 'I haven't exactly been consistent in my opinions.' He sighed, sitting back in his chair, although one of his arms remained draped across the back of hers. 'The truth is, I don't feel very consistent about anything at the moment!'

Tory felt the loss of his warm closeness, looking at him consideringly now. She had sensed from the first that something was troubling this man; she just wasn't sure how to go about getting him to talk about it. Or if indeed she should!

Jonathan was obviously even more self-contained than she was, and she doubted he would welcome any intrusion into what was, after all, a private matter. In fact, she knew that he wouldn't!

'It's very beautiful here,' he continued heavily, staring sightlessly in the direction of the shadowed hills.

'Very,' she agreed quietly. 'Healing, too,' she added.

Jonathan turned to give her a sharp look. 'And do you think I need healing?' His voice was edged with sarcasm now.

'I don't know. Do you?'

'Maybe.' He sighed heavily, standing up, taking his half-full glass of port with him as he strolled to the edge of the terrace. 'Until a couple of years ago I thought I knew who

I was, where I was going. Damn it, I didn't *think* I knew—
I *did* know!' He turned his head, his expression grim.

Tory watched him with narrowed eyes. 'What happened
a couple of years ago to change that...?' she prompted.

Jonathan turned back to her with glittering grey eyes.
'On the surface, absolutely nothing,' he bit out tersely.

'But below the surface?'

'Below the surface?' he repeated scathingly, his movements tense. 'I changed,' he revealed heavily. 'Believe it
or not, Tory, I've always been a very together type of person.'

Oh, she believed it. Just as she believed that something
had happened two years ago to make him less sure of himself, of where his life was going. Whether she now found
out what that something was all depended upon whether or
not he wanted to tell her...

'This is ridiculous!' he suddenly burst out, moving firmly
away from the edge of the terrace, turning back to look at
her. 'Here I am, having dinner with a woman millions of
men would crawl on their knees to be with—and all I can
find to entertain you with is my morose self-pity!' He shook
his head self-disgustedly.

Tory gave a wry smile. 'I think crawling on their knees
is probably a slight exaggeration!' Although one very determined male fan in Australia had once climbed up to the
sixth-floor balcony of her hotel room in an effort to meet
her!

Jonathan's gaze moved over her with warm appreciation.
'I don't,' he finally murmured huskily.

She couldn't meet that gaze, turning to look at the shadowed hills herself now. She had allowed this man to kiss
her, knew she had returned those kisses. She also knew it
was pure madness, on the part of both of them. In a few
days she would return to London, and eventually Jonathan

would return to America. Theirs was an attraction leading nowhere.

'Can I get you another glass of port?' Jonathan softly interrupted her troubled thoughts.

Considering she still had some in her glass—no.

She didn't find him in the least morose—wished he would tell her what was bothering him. Although she already knew him well enough to realise he wasn't a man who confided his troubles to anyone, least of all to a woman he had only known a few days!

'I don't think so, thanks.' She smiled her refusal, having enjoyed this evening in spite of her earlier misgivings. She glanced at the slender gold watch on her wrist, surprised to find it was almost eleven o'clock. 'It's late, and my father has to be up early in the morning.' So did she! 'I think I should give him a call so that he can come and get me—'

'It isn't even eleven o'clock yet,' Jonathan protested. 'I'll drive you home when you're ready to go.'

It wasn't a case of when she was ready to go; it would be all too easy to just stay here, to know the promise of passion his glittering grey gaze promised, to give Jonathan oblivion for a few hours from his obviously tortured thoughts. That would be oh, so easy to do—because it was what she wanted more than anything at this moment.

It was the thought of the two of them waking next to each other in the morning, of seeing the regret and self-disgust in Jonathan's face, that made even the idea of it impossible.

'I really think I should go now.' She put her glass down decisively on the table as she stood up. 'And I don't think it's a good idea for you to drive me home; there were half a dozen reporters at the end of the driveway when I left earlier.' She grimaced.

He shrugged. 'That doesn't bother me if it doesn't bother you.'

Were they back to the question of her being involved with someone else? Didn't Jonathan believe her when she told him she wasn't?

'Tory...?' He had closed the distance between them in two strides, one of his hands under her chin as he raised her face to his. 'I was referring to the fact that you're obviously here on holiday yourself,' he explained. 'A holiday that has obviously been ruined by the speculation concerning the two of us,' he added grimly.

'The same applies to you,' she reminded him.

'I'm not on holiday,' he told her harshly.

Tory frowned. If he wasn't here on holiday—? What possible work could he be doing here? More to the point, how could he be doing it at the Byrne house? She had suggested he go to the casino while he was here—a business he had told her his family was involved in—and he had very firmly refused to even consider it. So what was he doing here...?

She shook her head, knowing that if Jonathan had wanted to tell her then he would had done so.

'Do I take that as a no to my offer to drive you home?'

She looked up to find Jonathan watching her with narrowed eyes. She had been so deep in thought she hadn't realised he had been looking at her as she shook her head!

'Not at all,' she answered lightly. 'I'm sure my father will be only too pleased not to have to come out again this evening.' And maybe by now, believing that no one was going to leave the farmhouse again this evening, the reporters would have returned to whatever hotels they had booked into for the night! 'Thank you for dinner this evening, Jonathan. You obviously *can* cook!' she said mischievously.

'And I am forgiven for my rudeness to you earlier?'

Once again his closeness became overwhelming. In fact, he was so close to her Tory could once again feel the warmth emanating from his body. 'You're forgiven,' she confirmed huskily.

Jonathan became suddenly still, only his thumb moving caressingly against her lips now as he looked down at her with dark eyes. 'For some reason I'm very reluctant to let this evening end,' he said gruffly.

His words so echoed her previous thoughts that Tory couldn't repress the slight trembling she felt at the gentleness of his thumb against her lips. Although deep inside she ached for the caress of his lips against hers instead!

She swallowed hard. 'I think we both know that it has to,' she said quietly.

'Do we?'

She blinked, looking up at him uncertainly now. 'I think so.' But even to her own ears she didn't sound very convincing!

Jonathan tilted his head to one side as he looked at her consideringly. 'Would you spend the day with me tomorrow?' he asked.

Tory felt what was rapidly becoming a familiar leap of her heart inside her chest. 'I thought you came here to be alone,' she reminded him.

He gave a self-deriding laugh. 'Something else I've discovered since I came here—I'm not too happy with my own company any more!'

'In that case—' Tory grinned '—I suppose I had better rescue you from the boredom!'

Jonathan winced. 'Is that what my invitation sounded like? I'm sorry,' he muttered at her nod of confirmation. 'It wasn't meant like that at all.' He released her, standing back. 'Miss Buchanan, would you do me the honour of spending the day with me tomorrow? There, how was that?' he prompted teasingly.

'It will do,' she assured him dryly. 'And I would love to spend the day with you. What did you have in mind?' Even as she asked the question she could feel the hot colour entering her cheeks; her question had sounded provocative, to say the least!

Jonathan laughed huskily at her self-conscious grimace. Then he stopped laughing as suddenly as he had begun, tersely suggesting he drive her home now, as if the sound of his own laughter had come as something of a surprise to him.

Perhaps it had, Tory speculated as she sat beside him in the Jaguar on the drive back to the farm. Jonathan didn't give the impression he had found too much to laugh about for quite some time. Two years, in fact.

She couldn't help wondering what had happened then to bring about the changes in him that he had mentioned. It must have been something quite serious. Jonathan came over as a very self-confident, self-contained man. But something had happened two years ago that had changed that...

He had asked her earlier if there was already a romantic involvement in her life—perhaps she should have asked him the same question! At thirty-two or thirty-three, as she guessed him to be, it was very doubtful there hadn't been a serious involvement in his life to date. Maybe the breaking up of that involvement two years ago was what had affected the changes in him?

The realisation of that put something of a dampener on her agreement to spend the day with him tomorrow. If Jonathan was still suffering from the effects of a broken relationship two years later, then it must have been a very serious involvement. Perhaps she would be better to stay well away from him?

But it was too late to retract her decision now, without Jonathan demanding an explanation as to exactly why she was doing it. Besides, the part of her that trembled at his touch didn't really want to retract it!

Thankfully, the reporters seemed to have dispersed for the night. There was no sign of them as they turned down the driveway to her parents' house. The lights were still on in the downstairs rooms as Jonathan brought the car to a halt outside, meaning that both her parents had probably stayed up in anticipation of her call to be picked up.

But there was also a car she didn't recognise parked over by the garage...

'Thank you for a lovely evening,' she told Jonathan distractedly as he came round to open the car door for her, her attention still on the other unfamiliar car. Her parents hadn't mentioned expecting visitors this evening, and it wasn't a vehicle Tory recognised as being one of the family's.

'You're welcome,' Jonathan replied ruefully. 'What time shall I pick you up tomorrow?'

'I—' She was prevented from saying more as she heard the crunch of feet on gravel behind her, turning frowningly towards the sound. It had been a long time since her father had hauled her into the house at the end of a date because he considered she had arrived home too late!

'Tory, darling!' a familiar drawl greeted her, before a man stepped from the darkness at the side of the house into the light given off from inside the hallway.

But Tory had known exactly who it was before he did that, had recognised his voice the moment he spoke.

Rupert!

What was *he* doing here?

As she glanced at Jonathan, she could tell by his suddenly cold and bleak expression that he had taken one look at the other man—tall, loose-limbed, extremely good-looking Rupert—heard the way the other man had called her 'darling'—and drawn his own conclusions!

CHAPTER SEVEN

JUST as she could see from Rupert's suddenly speculative expression as he took in her appearance—Jonathan's arm protectively about her waist—that he had also drawn his own conclusions about the situation.

And from the way his expression darkened angrily she could see that he didn't like those conclusions one little bit!

'Darling...' he said again in that over-educated drawl that she had once found so attractive. 'Your parents have been extremely kind to me all evening, but I was beginning to think you were never coming home.' He grasped the tops of her arms before bending his head to kiss her lingeringly on the lips.

Tory at once felt Jonathan's arm leave her waist, whether deliberately or because Rupert had pulled her out of his grasp she wasn't sure.

One thing she was sure of—she did not like Rupert kissing her in this possessive way. In fact, she didn't like him kissing her, full stop!

She pulled sharply away from him, blue eyes glittering in the darkness. 'What are you doing here, Rupert?' she demanded.

He smiled unconcernedly before turning to look at Jonathan. 'As Tory's manners seem to have momentarily deserted her, I had better introduce myself,' he said, keeping a proprietorial hold on Tory's upper arm. 'Rupert Montgomery. And you must be Jonathan,' he added challengingly.

Grey eyes narrowed icily as Jonathan coldly returned the other man's gaze. 'Must I?'

'Oh, yes,' Rupert laughed confidently.

Tory was rigid with anger. Rupert was deliberately giving Jonathan the impression that he knew all about him—an impression Jonathan was obviously far from pleased about. Especially as the only person who could have provided that information was her...

'When did you get here, Rupert?' she demanded, irritably. '*How* did you get here?'

'It wasn't easy, believe me. I'm not sure the powers that be actually *want* visitors on this island,' he answered disparagingly. 'I had the devil of a job getting booked onto a flight this evening at all!'

So he had flown over this evening. But that still didn't tell her why...

'It's TT Fortnight,' Tory dismissed vaguely. 'What are you doing here, Rupert?' she repeated.

'Visiting you, of course,' he answered with brittle affection, his own arm lightly about her shoulders now.

A fact Jonathan wasn't unaware of, Tory noted angrily as she saw his gaze move coldly over their physical closeness. He had obviously assumed—with a lot of help from Rupert!—that her earlier denial of being involved with anyone was far from the truth.

She glared up at Rupert before moving pointedly away from him. 'Wasn't it assuming rather a lot to believe that I wanted a visit from you?' she responded rudely.

'I hope you'll excuse us, old boy.' Rupert smiled boyishly at Jonathan—a man who could only be three or four years his senior at most! 'I'm afraid Tory and I had a little tiff before she came to the island a week ago. Tory obviously still hasn't forgiven me.' He grimaced charmingly.

Apart from their height, the two men were so different,

Tory decided. Rupert had slightly over-long blond hair, laughing blue eyes, and was handsome to the point of male beauty. His body was slim and athletic—and that extreme handsomeness and boyish charm hid a completely selfish and calculating nature. Jonathan, on the other hand, was just as handsome in a darkly brooding way, also physically fit—and yet that arrogantly cold visage hid a much warmer nature, of a man who obviously cared very deeply about his family.

Of the two, Tory knew which one she preferred!

'There's nothing to forgive, Rupert,' she replied. 'You have your ideas on where my future lies, and I have mine— they just happen to be in opposite directions!' She drew in a deeply controlling breath before turning to look at Jonathan. 'I really did enjoy this evening,' she told him, blue gaze pleading for a softening of his coldly set features.

There wasn't one. If anything, his mouth had taken on an even grimmer look. 'You're welcome,' he bit out tersely. 'And now I think I had better leave and let you and—Mr Montgomery—sort out your differences,' he added with a contemptuous curl of his top lip.

Her 'differences' with Rupert were rapidly becoming insurmountable, Tory was quickly realising. Just as she realised exactly what impression Rupert was deliberately giving Jonathan about their relationship. He was making them sound like a couple of star-crossed lovers who had had a silly argument!

She reached out and placed her hand on Jonathan's arm, her fingers tightening as she felt him tense. 'What time shall I meet you tomorrow?' she enquired huskily; after all, he had invited her to spend the day with him. And some time during that day she would find the right time to explain exactly what her 'differences' with Rupert were!

Jonathan raised dark brows, his gaze flickering briefly

over Rupert before coming back to rest mockingly on Tory's upturned face. 'Let's take a raincheck, hmm?' he suggested. 'I'm sure you're going to be—busy, for the next few days. With your guest,' he added with sarcasm.

Rupert was not her guest—a fact he was very quickly going to realise for himself once Jonathan had left, in spite of what arrangements her polite parents might have otherwise assumed!

With a last regretful look at Jonathan's unrelenting expression she removed her hand from his arm. 'Perhaps you're right,' she accepted. 'Enjoy the rest of your stay,' she added evenly.

He gave a sharp inclination of his head before turning to Rupert. 'Montgomery,' he barked, before striding back to his car and getting inside without so much as a backward glance, much to Tory's dismay.

She watched Jonathan drive away, tensing resentfully as Rupert moved to stand at her side, his arm once again moving possessively about her shoulders.

Tory gave an angry shrug to shake off that arm, turning to glare at Rupert once the Jaguar lights had disappeared down the driveway. 'What do you think you're doing?' she asked Rupert furiously.

He looked totally unconcerned, raising blond brows in mocking amusement. 'So that was the elusive Jonathan...' he drawled.

She stiffened. 'Yes?'

'Don't tell you actually find him attractive, Tory,' Rupert scorned. 'The man's like a block of ice.'

Angry colour darkened her cheeks. 'When I want your opinion, Rupert, I'll ask for it! Goodnight.' She turned and strode off towards the farmhouse.

Gravel once again crunched underfoot as Rupert followed her. 'Your parents have invited me to stay the night,' he informed her lightly, his satisfaction with the arrangement clearly audible in his voice.

Tory stopped before opening the back door, turning on her heel to glare at him. 'And I just uninvited you,' she bit out.

He gave a movement of his shoulders, as if puzzled by her unrelenting attitude. 'Isn't that a little rude of you?' he cajoled.

As if she were a child who needed humouring, Tory decided resentfully. 'Call it what you like, Rupert,' she rejoined. 'There are plenty of hotels in Douglas. Admittedly you may have a little trouble getting booked into one this time of year, but you could always try asking one of the TT fans if you can share their tent for the night!' she added with relish, suddenly having a wonderful vision of Rupert in his designer-label clothes having to camp out in a tent. Just the idea of it made her feel more cheerful!

Had she really once thought herself in love with this man? she inwardly chided herself. He was nothing more than an overgrown public schoolboy with a penchant for nice clothes and a comfortable lifestyle.

Something she, with her recent decision to re-evaluate her career, was obviously threatening...

Strange, but until a few months ago she had thought she owed the success of her career to Rupert. A deliberate illusion on Rupert's part, she could now see with hindsight. Because actually it had always been the other way around. Which was why Rupert had suddenly become so attentive. Even to the point of asking her to marry him...

Which brought her neatly round to what she knew had to be the real reason Rupert had hot-footed it over to the island this evening; he had obviously found the reference in the newspapers to her mystery male companion of Sunday night a little too disturbing for comfort. His own!

How it must have annoyed him to arrive here this evening only to find her out once again with the mysterious Jonathan!

Rupert looked irritated now. 'That isn't funny, Tory.'

'No?' she raised dark brows. 'Strange—I find it highly amusing!'

He reached out and grasped her arm as she would have opened the farmhouse door. 'Don't you think you're being a little unfair to your parents?' he pointed out in a hushed voice. Her parents were obviously sitting in the kitchen, where they might inadvertently overhear this heated conversation. 'After all, they were polite enough to make the invitation. It's going to be a little awkward if you now tell them I'm going to a hotel instead.'

'Awkward for whom?' she challenged, although inwardly she had to concede that he had a point. Her parents were going to think Rupert didn't consider their farm good enough for him if he now did an about-face and left to stay in a hotel...

'Stop being childish, Tory.' Rupert sighed his impatience with her attitude. 'It's almost midnight; I can hardly turn up at a hotel at this time of night!'

She arched dark brows. 'I don't remember it stopping you before,' she reminded him softly.

'Back to that, are we?' Blue eyes narrowed dangerously as his charming façade totally slipped. 'I told you, I was upset because you were making me wait before giving me an answer to my marriage proposal—'

'So upset you picked up a woman at the after-show party and took her back to your hotel room for the night!' Tory finished disgustedly.

Although she wasn't sure who she was most disgusted with. Herself, for actually having been considering that marriage proposal. Or Rupert, because she obviously meant so little to him he had gone to bed with someone else on the same night he'd asked her to marry him!

Not that she had needed that extra proof of the shallowness of his feelings for her, but it hadn't stopped it rankling, nonetheless...

'Oh, let's just forget that, Rupert,' she dismissed. 'I suppose if my parents have asked you to stay, and you've already accepted, then you had better stay. But I want you to leave first thing in the morning,' she added firmly as his expression lightened with triumph.

'Deal,' he accepted readily.

Too readily, Tory knew from experience. Rupert was obviously hoping that in the light of day she would relent in her attitude. He was in for a disappointment!

Not that any of that showed as she let them both back into the farmhouse kitchen, her smile light and natural as she answered her parents' questions about her evening. There was no point in unduly worrying them with the problem of Rupert. It was a problem she would ultimately have to deal with herself.

After this evening, she had a feeling it was going to be sooner rather than later!

But at the moment her more immediate problem was Jonathan. They had spent an enjoyable evening together, had arranged to meet again tomorrow—and Rupert's untimely arrival had put an end to all that.

When *would* she see Jonathan again?

More to the point, would she see him again *at all*...!

'Thought I'd find you here,' Rupert said happily as he let himself into her music studio.

Tory barely spared him a glance, concentrating as she was on her guitar work. She was trying to remember the haunting tune Jonathan had been playing last Sunday evening. She had most of what she had heard, but it wasn't complete. And she still didn't know if it had any words to go with it...

Rupert strolled unconcernedly across the room to stand next to where she sat on the sofa. 'Hmm, pretty.' He nodded as she continued to pick out the notes. 'Something new you're working on?' he prompted at her lack of response to his first remark.

'Something like that,' she replied, still not sparing him a glance.

'Your mother has just given me the most enormous breakfast,' he said with satisfaction. 'Perhaps there's something to be said for living off the land, after all.'

Tory's mouth twisted. 'The eggs are fresh, but as we don't keep pigs the bacon came from the supermarket, and my mother stopped baking her own bread years ago, so the same applies to your toast!'

He arched blond brows. 'A little pedantic this morning, aren't we?'

Tory was learning to feel extremely irritated by that lightly cajoling voice! 'Just being honest,' she responded. 'Now, as you've already noticed, I'm busy. So if you have nothing of real importance to say...?'

Rupert's answer to that was to drop down onto the sofa beside her. Tory had no choice but to look at him. As usual, Rupert was impeccably dressed—silvery-grey trousers teamed with a pale grey shirt, his shoes hand-made highly polished black leather. Very suitable attire for wearing on a working farm!

His brows rose ruefully as he saw her assessing glance. 'I can always learn,' he murmured softly.

'Why bother?' she said, not pretending to misunderstand his reference as she stood up to put her guitar back on its stand, very slim in fitted blue denims and a blue tee shirt.

'You won't be staying long,' she assured him firmly as she turned to face him.

'I can't believe you're still angry with me, Tory,' he drawled, not in the least perturbed by her attitude. 'After all, you've apparently been having a minor fling with America's answer to Heathcliff, and you don't see me sulking about it.'

She glared across at him, disliking intensely his description of Jonathan. 'I haven't been having a fling with anyone, minor or otherwise. And even if I had, you aren't sulking about it because, as we both know, you have no right to do so!'

'I have asked you to marry me, Tory,' he reminded her huskily.

'"Tory"?' she repeated mockingly, Rupert having always insisted in the past upon calling her by her full name, Victory. 'And you may have asked, Rupert—but as I recall you have also been given the very firm answer of no!'

He looked at her. 'You were angry at the time—'

Having arrived at his hotel room several weeks ago to be greeted by a very disheveled redhead wearing only a bathtowel, was that so surprising?

'Well, I'm not angry now—and the answer is still no!' she told him emphatically. 'In fact—'

'You know, Victory,' he drawled pointedly, 'you are fast developing a prima donna's temper.'

Her mouth snapped shut at the insult, twin wings of colour in her cheeks as she glared at him.

'In fact,' Rupert continued mercilessly, 'you are becoming the proverbial temperamental pain in the butt!'

'I— You—'

'What's the matter, Victory?' he taunted. 'Or is it that you can't stand hearing the truth about yourself?'

Was it the truth? Had she become one of those egotistical

bores that she had met at so many parties over the last five years? People who could talk of nothing but themselves, and had no interest in anything that wasn't going to further their own career?

Had she…?

'It isn't easy for me to say these things to you, Victory,' Rupert continued, moving closer to her on the sofa, his arm along its back. 'But someone has to do it.'

And it might as well be him! Basically because he was enjoying doing it, Tory knew.

But that wasn't what was important at the moment. Had she become one of those people who believed in their own publicity to such a degree that they became totally selfish and self-motivated?

She looked searchingly into Rupert's handsome face. His expression was bland, blue gaze non-committal.

No, she wasn't like that at all! Rupert was the one who operated on that self-orientated system!

To the point that he would lie to her to achieve his own aims…?

Absolutely, yes!

Her mouth twisted wryly. 'Nice try, Rupert,' she came back at him mockingly. 'You almost had me hooked into believing you again for a moment. Instead of which—' she stood up, looking down at him with cold blue eyes '—you have just finally made my mind up for me. Don't make any more bookings for me other than the ones I'm already committed to—I have other plans now!'

'I've already warned you. You simply can't take a year out at this juncture in your career!' he hissed furiously, sitting tensely forward on the sofa as he looked up at her with glacial eyes.

'Careful, Rupert, your charm is slipping,' Tory taunted.

'Damn my charm!' He stood up in one forcefully fluid movement.

Tory stood her ground. 'My sentiments exactly,' she replied scathingly. 'We had a five-year contract, Rupert,' she told him harshly, pointed chin raised defiantly. 'With an option to renew on both sides at the end of that time. That contract comes to an end in three months' time, fortuitously at the end of the European tour. At which time we will definitely be parting company—personally as well as professionally!'

Cold fury made his narrowed eyes glitter icily. 'You won't last six months without me,' Rupert said nastily, his mouth turned back in a sneer.

In truth, Tory was shaking so badly after her announcement that she had to grasp her hands tightly together in front of her to prevent him from seeing how affected she was.

But, having made the statement, she felt a curious sense of calm spreading through her.

She had enjoyed most of the last five years—the last three of them well at the top of the music tree. But a lot of time lately had been taken up with recordings, the release of albums, appearances on television shows, chat shows. Her personal performances to the audience she loved the best, the fans who went out and actually bought her CDs, were becoming less and less as Rupert involved her more and more in the incestuous world of show business.

'I made you what you are!' Rupert could stand her silence no longer, his face an angry mask, hands clenched into fists at his sides.

'Now that is a bare-faced lie.' Tory shook her head pityingly. 'You helped guide my career. I accept that, and I'm grateful for it—'

'You have a funny way of showing it!' he ground out harshly.

She arched dark brows. 'I am grateful for it, Rupert,' she repeated firmly. 'But you didn't give me the voice that I have—'

'Neither did those two simple souls over there!' He nodded his head in the direction of the farmhouse.

Tory's eyes flashed deeply blue. 'You're going too far, Rupert,' she warned him in a hushed voice, her face very white.

His mouth twisted viciously. 'Why? Because I've dared to mention the fact that the Buchanans aren't your natural parents?' He shook his head scathingly. 'Because, with a birthday in mid-March, you're probably the result of some brief encounter at one of this island's famous TT gatherings?'

Tory's hands were no longer shaking from reaction but from anger—raw, almost uncontrollable anger. Almost. Because that was what Rupert wanted. To hurt her so much she completely lost it. But he was going about it all the wrong way if he thought insulting her parentage—or lack of it!—was going to result in that.

It had never bothered her that she was adopted. She knew that no one could have loved her as much as Thelma and Dan Buchanan, or given her the belief in herself that had allowed her the freedom six years ago to follow her dream.

No, Rupert could never hurt her with the fact that she was adopted. Or with disparaging remarks about who her real parents might be. But he could evoke extreme anger in her by casting any slight on the two people who had *chosen* to be her parents!

'I think you had better go, Rupert,' she told him wearily. 'Before you say something we'll both regret.'

'Oh?' he sneered.

'Oh.' She nodded, meeting his furious gaze unblinkingly.

He drew in a controlling breath, obviously dampening down his own anger with extreme effort. 'Let's not fall out about this, Tory.' His voice had softened to that gentle cajoling again as he realised he really had gone too far. 'We have too much history together to argue now. If you're really set on taking this year out—'

'At least a year, Rupert,' she put in determinedly. 'And I sincerely hope the history you're referring to is our professional one,' she continued tautly, her own anger far from defused. 'Any personal involvement—such as it was!—ended long ago.' Her head went back in challenge.

His mouth curved into a rueful smile. 'I take it that's another no to my marriage proposal?'

He had realised that anger wasn't going to achieve anything, and the charm was on its way back, Tory accepted. But it was too late for that. Far too late!

'I haven't changed my mind from three weeks ago,' she said dully, knowing that where Rupert was concerned she never would. 'My advice to you now is go back to London, and I'll join you there for the start of the tour.'

He moved closer to her. 'Promise?'

Once again Tory stood her ground. 'I have never reneged on a commitment to my fans, and I'm not about to start now!' Even if the thought of spending any length of time in Rupert's company made her flesh creep.

She had realised—too slowly, she acknowledged self-disgustedly—that Rupert was a completely selfish swine, but he had never before personally attacked her parents in the way he had today. That—especially after he had just enjoyed their warm hospitality—she found unforgivable.

She knew that he would use every occasion he could over the next three months to try and get her to change her mind about renewing her contract with him as her manager. It was going to be a very trying three months...!

'Let's go and see if we can get you booked on a flight off the island today,' she said briskly. 'It's much easier to get off than it is on at the moment,' she added. There was racing today and Friday still to come before TT was over for another year.

She was right, and managed to get Rupert booked on an afternoon flight back to Heathrow. She refused to drive him to the airport, ordering him a taxi instead and using the excuse—if she needed one!—that the roads would be clogged enough already this afternoon, with the races on, without having to fight her way back through it as well.

Rupert paused at the open taxi door, his luggage stowed in the boot, the driver already inside, waiting for him to get in the back of the car. 'I'm sorry I lost my temper this morning,' he told Tory quietly.

She was sure that he was. Oh, not because he regretted hurting her with the things that he had said, but because he knew he had simply gone too far.

'So am I,' she said, sounding tired. 'But at least we both know where we stand now.'

Rupert gave a heavy sigh, reaching up to gently cup one side of her face with his hand. 'If it's any consolation, you're the only person that can make me completely lose control like that.' He gave a sad grimace.

That was only because, as the manager of Victory Canan, he had managed to command a lot of respect over the years, and he had wielded that power to his own advantage. In fact, very few people ever stood up to him and said no. If they did, they didn't last very long. It must be galling him very badly at the moment that it was Tory herself who was thwarting him. Besides, with her refusal to keep him on as her manager, she would be removing the power he had wielded so effectively for himself...!

'It isn't,' she replied. 'I— What—?' Her words were abruptly cut off as Rupert suddenly pulled her hard against him, his lips coming down possessively on hers as he moulded her body against his.

What on earth was he doing?

Tory pushed against him. Completely ineffectively. His arms felt like steel bands around her. Damn it, with his easy lifestyle, his love of good food and even better wines, she hadn't realised he could be this physically domineering!

As the kiss went on and on—for what seemed like an eternity because she wasn't enjoying it in the least!—Tory became aware of something else. The sound of a car coming down the gravel driveway...

At last Rupert lifted his head, his expression momentarily triumphant as he looked down at her briefly before turning in the direction of the sound of that approaching car.

A Jaguar.

And a thunderous-faced Jonathan McGuire was sitting behind the wheel...!

CHAPTER EIGHT

TORY turned accusingly back to Rupert, not fooled for a moment by that innocently questioning raise of blond brows. 'You did that on purpose,' she ground out angrily as she heard the Jaguar come to a halt on the gravel several feet behind her.

Rupert grinned down at her unrepentantly. 'I seem to remember you told me Jonathan had left the island. All's fair in love and war, and all that,' he said with satisfaction.

Her mouth firmed. 'As there is absolutely no love between us, I think we just declared war,' she muttered, before turning as she heard the Jaguar car door open and then slam shut.

Jonathan was out of the car now, wearing faded denims and a black tee shirt, sunglasses hiding those normally very expressive grey eyes. But it was obvious from the thin line of his mouth that his mood hadn't improved at all from last night!

Why should it have done? He had just arrived to see her in what looked like a very passionate clinch with Rupert!

'Jonathan,' she greeted him warmly, stepping determinedly away from Rupert's light hold on her. 'You've arrived just in time to say goodbye to Rupert before he catches his plane home,' she announced very pointedly.

'Business commitments,' Rupert put in.

Jonathan turned his head slightly, and Tory could only assume he was looking at the younger man; those dark glasses were a very effective shield. 'Goodbye, Rupert,' he said uninterestedly.

'Jonathan.' Rupert nodded, still looking extremely pleased with himself.

As well he might, Tory inwardly fumed. He had been aware of Jonathan's approach in the Jaguar several minutes before she had, which was why he had been treated to that so-called passionate display.

Rupert would pay for that one later, she decided, smiling at Jonathan now. 'Would you like to come in for coffee?' she invited smoothly, determined to make sure Rupert left with the distinct impression his deliberate sabotage of any relationship she might or might not have with Jonathan hadn't worked.

Even if it had! She and Jonathan, she knew, had reached some sort of understanding last night—a fragile admission of an attraction between them, if nothing else. Rupert's un-expected arrival had damaged that. His deliberate display of possessive passion just now had magnified the situation.

'Sure,' Jonathan accepted brusquely. 'Don't let us keep you, Montgomery; as Tory said, you have a plane to catch.'

Rupert gave Tory a brightly unconcerned smile. 'I'll call you as soon as I get back to London.'

'Don't trouble yourself,' she told him tightly. 'If you go missing, it will be on the six o'clock news!'

Rupert chuckled unconcernedly. 'She's such a joker,' he told the other man appreciatively.

'I wasn't joking,' Tory muttered out the side of her mouth, so that only Rupert could hear.

'I know,' he muttered back, lightly pinching her arm be-fore sliding into the back of the taxi and closing the door.

Tory bent down to the open window. 'Do give my love to Pamela, won't you?' she told him tauntingly.

Rupert's mouth tightened at the mention of the name of the woman who had shared his hotel room three weeks ago. 'I haven't seen her since that night,' he grated, obviously aware of Jonathan, standing only feet away, even if the other man couldn't now hear their hushed conversation.

'Lucky Pamela,' Tory opined.

Rupert looked up at her with narrowed eyes. 'You know, I'm not taking our earlier discussion as an end to that particular subject,' he warned grimly.

She shrugged. 'That is, of course, up to you—but I can assure you, from my point of view, it's well and truly at an end.' Her decision made, she would now stick to it. The irony of it was, it had been Rupert's hounding of her that had made the decision all the easier to make!

She had been approached several months ago by a world-famous producer to star in his new show, which he hoped to put on in London in six months' time, with the added incentive that, as the female lead was actually a singer, Tory could also write the songs that she was to perform.

At the time she had politely thanked Stephen James for the offer but explained she wasn't an actress, that he would be better advised to offer the part to someone who was. But Stephen, bless him, hadn't been willing to accept no for an answer, had explained that he had written the part with her in mind.

Despite her misgivings—after all, she was a singer, nothing else!—Tory couldn't deny she'd been flattered by the offer, and the possibility that she just might be able to do it had begun to grow and then blossom in her mind.

Much to Rupert's disgust. There was no money in it, he had warned her. She would be totally tied to London for the foreseeable future, appearing in the theatre six nights a week until goodness knew when.

But Tory had already known all that, and none of those reasons accounted for her hesitation. She simply didn't want to let Stephen James or her own fans down.

On the plus side of it, however, was the new challenge—

a chance to see if she could be more than she already was. And, after five years at the top of her profession, she acknowledged she was ready for that change. It would also free her, once and for all, from the domineering Rupert...

'We'll see about that once you get back to London,' Rupert told her grimly now, before tapping the taxi-driver on the shoulder and telling him to drive him to the airport.

Tory turned to Jonathan once the taxi had gone, smiling brightly even though she received no answering smile. 'Coffee?' she reminded him.

He gave an abrupt inclination of his head, following her into the farmhouse kitchen. 'Your parents aren't here this afternoon?' he prompted tersely once he had sat down at the table.

Tory's movements were economically efficient as she poured them both a mug of coffee from the constantly fresh brew in the pot. 'Dad has taken my mother to have a checkup on her ankle. Why?' She quirked dark brows as she sat across the table from him. 'Are you frightened to be here alone with me?' She deliberately mocked the image Victory Canan had of being a vamp.

'Hardly,' he dismissed scathingly. 'I telephoned earlier on my mobile before driving back from Ramsey and got the answer-machine again, that's all. Obviously your parents aren't here to answer any calls, and you— Well, you were obviously otherwise engaged!' he observed with pointed scorn.

With Rupert, his derisive tone implied! 'Did you telephone for anything specific?' Tory queried sarcastically. 'Or was it just a social call?' Although what could possibly have been so urgent on a social level that he'd had to telephone on his mobile from Ramsey—a town seven miles away in the north of the island—she just couldn't imagine!

'No, it damn well—!' Jonathan drew in a sharply controlling breath as he broke off the angry reply.

The silence that followed felt just as uncomfortable, Tory decided a few minutes later. What was the matter with the man? He had made it more than obvious the night before that she wouldn't be seeing him today, as planned, and now it turned out that not only had he telephoned earlier, but had actually come over here when he'd received no answer to his call...

The man was in constant contradiction of his own decisions! He had told her when he'd arrived here that he wanted to be alone, and yet he had been to the farm several times in the last four days—had invited her over to his sister's house, too. Now he had arrived here again, after telling her he would take a raincheck on their date for today. She couldn't keep up with the man's unpredictability!

Tory gave a heavy sigh of her own. 'I don't understand you, Jonathan—'

'Nor I you!' He stood up, his chair scraping noisily on the mellow tiled floor as he glared down at her. 'That man—Montgomery—' his mouth turned back in a sneer '—he obviously has some sort of proprietorial claim on you—'

'He's my manager, if you really want to know!' This accusing attitude, after Rupert's recent duplicity, was just too much. Tory glared straight back up at Jonathan as he towered over her.

'Really?' he parried.

'Yes—really!' She couldn't believe they were having this conversation. If she hadn't known Jonathan better, she might have said he was jealous of Rupert—and God knew that was what Rupert had hoped for! Except she *did* know Jonathan better...

He gave a humourless smile. 'And it's obvious in what way he "manages" you!'

'Why, you—!' Tory stood up herself now, striding furiously around the table, her arm raised, ready to swing.

Jonathan easily caught hold of it. He pushed her arm back down to her side, long fingers moving down to become entwined with her own, bringing her body up close to his in the process.

His face was very close to hers as they glared at each other. 'Looking at you now, your eyes flashing, face flushed—albeit with anger—I could easily give in to the temptation to manage you myself,' he ground out grimly

'Try it,' Tory muttered, mouth firm, her chin jutting out.

His fingers tightened against hers before he gently bent her arm against her back, his body now moulded against hers. Making Tory fully aware of the truth of his words, his body was obviously aroused.

As her own was rapidly becoming! The warmth and smell of Jonathan set her senses reeling, and her breathing was suddenly shallow as she looked up at the sensuous curve of his mouth.

Longing for it to take possession of hers?

Oh, yes! She wanted Jonathan in a way she had never wanted any man before; she only had to be near him to know that.

But what did he want?

Her, obviously. But what for? A brief fling—as Rupert had called it? Or something more?

Don't be a fool, Tory, she instantly answered herself. Jonathan was a man with obvious troubles of his own. The sort of troubles, she believed, that meant at this time in his life he didn't have the time or space for any other feelings.

Yet he *did* want her...

As she wanted him...!

His free hand moved up to cup one side of her face, fingers curving about her jaw as he held her still to receive his kiss. A fierce, demanding kiss that robbed Tory of the ability to breathe.

Drowning must be like this, Tory decided dreamily as the kiss went on and on, her breath totally gone, a hazy darkness taking over, heightening her senses to an awareness of touch only.

Jonathan felt so good against her caressing hand—his back hard and muscled, shoulders wide, his hair like silk against her fingertips as they became entwined in its darkness.

Jonathan released her hand now, curving her body more intimately with his, his hands moving restlessly against the slenderness of her back.

It wasn't enough, Tory acknowledged achingly. Not nearly enough!

Her breath left her in a sigh of pure pleasure as one of those long, tapered hands moved to cup her breast, easily searching out her roused nipple, stroking its sensitivity as Tory groaned low in her throat.

Her legs felt weak, her head swam. She was aware only of the deep pulsing pleasure of Jonathan's caressing hands. Until she felt the touch of his lips against her bared flesh...!

She had never known pleasure like this. Heat was coursing through her body, every part of her feeling like a liquid flame as she lay limply against him.

His tongue moved moistly against the fiery tip now, circling, teeth lightly biting, before moving silkily against her once again, until Tory began to feel she would explode from the heated pleasure.

'Jonathan, I—' She didn't get to finish what she had been about to say, suddenly finding herself put firmly away from him, her tee shirt pulled down over her throbbing breasts.

He swore darkly to himself, running an agitated hand through his already tousled hair.

Tousled from her own fingers running through its darkness, she acknowledged dully.

Why had Jonathan stopped so suddenly? Why had he put her away from him like that? What—?

'I heard a car outside,' he said grimly as if in answer to her inward query. 'It's probably your parents returning from the doctor's.'

It probably was, Tory accepted, although she had been unaware of any car arriving outside herself.

Because she had been totally lost in the desire Jonathan had evoked in her!

Although if Jonathan had heard the car he couldn't have been as absorbed in passion as she had been...

He looked up impatiently from buttoning his shirt—the shirt Tory must have undone in her arousal! 'Perhaps you had better go upstairs and put on something a little less— revealing, before your parents come in,' he bit out abruptly, giving a pointed glance towards her breasts.

Tory looked down at herself, easily able to see the reason for his concern; her breasts were jutting forward beneath the tee shirt, her nipples still obviously aroused.

As she was herself, though her brain was still befuddled from the passion she and Jonathan had just shared. At least...she had thought they shared it; looking at Jonathan now—his shirt rebuttoned, his hair smoothed back to some semblance of order, his expression grim—it was hard to imagine he had been involved in anything more than drinking a cup of coffee in the last ten minutes!

Jonathan took her firmly by the shoulders and turned her in the direction of the hallway. 'Just go, Tory,' he ordered. 'I'll keep your parents busy here until you come back down.'

Tory stumbled obediently from the room and up the stairs to her bedroom, leaning weakly back against the door as she heard her parents' entrance downstairs, their obvious surprise at finding Jonathan alone in the kitchen.

What had happened just now?

Jonathan had made love to her, and she had undoubtedly responded! But had Jonathan?

Oh, he had been aroused; that was undeniable. But had that arousal come from passion, or had there still been an underlying angry edge to it? Because of what he believed to be her intimate relationship with Rupert?

Of course there had, she berated herself with a self-disgusted groan. Hadn't Jonathan told her before he'd kissed her that he wanted to 'manage' her in the same way Rupert obviously did!

And she had responded anyway! Because she'd wanted to. Because anger had been the last thing on her mind when she was in Jonathan's arms.

She was a fool. A stupid, romantic fool—

Romantic…?

She swallowed hard, feeling the colour drain from her face.

She was in love with Jonathan McGuire…!

How on earth—? Why—? How—?

She walked over to her bed to sink weakly down on top of the duvet. She was in love with Jonathan. It didn't matter why or how—it was a fact!

Well, you've done some pretty stupid things in your time, Tory Buchanan, she chided herself, but this must be the crowning glory of them all!

She could hear the murmur of voices down in the kitchen now as her parents talked with Jonathan. How could she go down there now, behave in the least normally, when she had just realised her love for him?

But, alternatively, how could she *not* go down? Her parents must already think it odd that she hadn't been in the kitchen with their guest when they'd arrived home—although she was sure the more than capable Jonathan would have come up with a feasible explanation for that! She would have to go down, and very shortly, too.

How was she going to face Jonathan again? It would have been bad enough after the way she had melted so passionately in his arms, without the added humiliation of realising she actually loved the man!

But he didn't know she loved him...

Of course he didn't, she told herself briskly. She had responded to him, yes; there could be no denying that. But she hadn't actually told him how she felt about him.

She never would, she decided as she changed her tee shirt for a loose blue denim shirt. There was simply no point in him ever knowing. He certainly didn't love her. But he would only be on the island a few more days at most. There was no reason why the two of them should be alone together again during that time. She would have to make sure they weren't; there was simply no future for them together. She could deal with the problem of her un-requited love once Jonathan had gone back to America...

She could hear the sound of her parents laughing with Jonathan as she approached the kitchen a few minutes later, fighting down the ridiculous feelings of jealousy their shared humour evoked. Jonathan had a whole life in America that she knew nothing about; she couldn't be jealous of everything and everyone else that in any way shared a part of his life!

'Okay, love?' her father prompted as she entered the kitchen. Her parents were sitting down at the kitchen table with Jonathan, steaming mugs of coffee in front of them.

'You didn't burn yourself, did you?' Her father frowned his concern.

Tory shook her head, shooting Jonathan a questioning glance; exactly what explanation had he given her parents for her absence when they'd got home?

'Are you sure?' Jonathan stood up now, coming over to join her where she still stood in the open doorway. 'The coffee was still pretty hot when you spilt it down yourself,' he added pointedly.

So that was the explanation. Pretty good. As lies went! It even covered the fact that she was dressed differently from when her parents left the house…!

'I'm absolutely fine,' she dismissed, avoiding Jonathan's probing gaze as she brushed past him. 'How did you get on at the doctor's, Mum?' Her legs were shaking, her face felt fiery-red, and she was sure her eyes were overbright. She couldn't look directly at Jonathan as she still felt the intentness of that silver gaze on her, but at least she was here, trying to appear normal. Whether or not she was succeeding was another matter entirely!

'Fine.' Her mother grimaced, giving her freshly bandaged ankle a disapproving look. 'I'm still more annoyed at the inconvenience than I am anything else.' She shook her head, smiling ruefully. 'Never mind, love. The doctor said I should be able to get around a lot better by the time you have to leave on Monday.'

'You're leaving?' Jonathan echoed curtly.

Tory shot him another glance. And then wished she hadn't. Just the sight of his grimly handsome face was enough to make her heart leap in her chest and quicken her pulse-rate. The man didn't even need to touch her to have a devastating effect on her. How on earth was she going to be able to stand this?

'As my mother just said,' she confirmed, giving a mocking inclination of her head.

Jonathan looked at her through narrowed lids, a look that it took great effort of will on Tory's part to withstand. But she mustn't by word or gesture, ever let this man know how she felt about him. It would be too humiliating.

He drew in a harsh breath, obviously completely dissatisfied with whatever he could read from her expression. 'Once again, I thank you for your hospitality,' he said shortly. 'I had better be going now. I have some shopping in the car I need to get home and put in the refrigerator.'

That hadn't seemed to bother him fifteen minutes ago, Tory thought uncharitably. Goodness, she was becoming as contradictory as this man was; on the one hand she couldn't wait for him to leave, and on the other she was angry with him for wanting to! Was this what being in love felt like? If it was, she was glad she had never felt the emotion before!

'Would you walk out to the car with me?'

Tory blinked as she realised Jonathan was talking to her. Walk out to the car with him? What on earth for? But then, with a sickening jolt of her stomach, she knew; Jonathan wanted to make sure she knew that what had happened between them a short time ago had meant nothing to him.

Her mouth set mutinously. 'Of course,' she agreed shortly, ignoring the speculative glances passing between her parents as she preceded Jonathan outside.

But she was aware of Jonathan directly behind her as she walked over to the Jaguar, could feel the heat of his body, the intensity of his gaze somewhere in the vicinity of her shoulder blades.

She turned once she reached the car, unable to look at his face for fear of what she might see there. Anger? Mockery? Pity...? Her gaze fixed on the third button down on his shirt. A button she had so recently undone so that she could touch the warm flesh beneath—

No! She mustn't think of that. It would get her nowhere to think of the passion so recently between them. Would only cause her pain.

'Tory—' He broke off abruptly as she flinched from the hand he had raised to touch her cheek. 'Hey, I'm not going to do anything to hurt you!' he rasped harshly.

Just being near him at this particular moment was hurting her! Maybe once she had got used to the idea of loving him, had come to terms with the futility of it, she might be able to at least be in the same room as him without cringing with embarrassment. As it was, she couldn't be near him like this, let alone let him actually touch her!

'Of course you aren't.' She smiled up at him brightly, although she was still unable to meet his gaze.

'Then why—? Never mind,' he dismissed impatiently. 'Tory, I think we need to talk—'

'We are talking,' she cut in hardly, wishing he would just leave.

Perhaps she would be successful as an actress, after all— she was managing to stand here, behaving quite normally, when what she really wanted to do was escape back up to her bedroom and lick her wounds in private!

'Polite niceties because your parents are nearby,' Jonathan protested. 'I meant really talk, Tory.'

She had managed to raise her gaze to the level of that arrogantly jutting chin, could just see his mouth, too. But there was nothing he could say that she wanted to hear from the grimly set line of his lips.

'Some other time, Jonathan.' She gave a careless wave of her hand.

'You—'

'I thought you were in a hurry to put your shopping in the fridge,' she reminded him tautly.

'That was merely an excuse to speak to you alone, and you know it—'

'Do I?' she demanded. 'Well, if you say so.' She gestured unconcernedly.

He drew in a harshly frustrated breath. 'You're being deliberately obtuse—'

'And you are intent on making something out of nothing!' she came back fiercely, glaring straight up into his face now. 'Things got a little—out of hand, earlier. Or do I mean the opposite?' She paused, and then continued, 'It happens. There's no need to make a federal case out of it!'

'"It happens"?' he repeated disgustedly. 'Well, it doesn't happen to me!' he bit out coldly. 'If your parents hadn't returned when they did then we would most likely have ended up making love on the kitchen floor!'

Would they? Tory felt a warm quiver down her spine just at the thought of it.

'Uncomfortable, granted,' she came back coolly, to hide that quiver. 'But not the end of the world, surely?' she added challengingly.

Nowhere near the end of the world as far as she was concerned; to have made love with Jonathan, completely, passionately, would perhaps have been a good memory to look back on when the pain of loving him hurt too much.

Despite what he might think to the contrary, it would have been her very first experience of lovemaking. She hadn't been brought up in a family where brief affairs were part of the norm, had grown up knowing that love was the vital ingredient of a physically loving relationship. The only man she had been close to for any length of time during the last five years had been Rupert, and she had never intended to become just another notch on *his* already very full bedpost!

Not that she thought Jonathan would ever believe that. Although if he had made love to her he would have been left in no doubt; her virginity was an undeniable fact!

Maybe it was as well they hadn't made love, kitchen floor or elsewhere—otherwise how much more intense this post-lovemaking conversation would have been!

'Don't give it another thought, Jonathan,' she replied carelessly. 'Emotions were running a little high, that's all. We were more angry with each other than anything,' she qualified, with some truth.

'Maybe,' he accepted. 'And maybe you're right. We should just forget it ever happened.' He opened the car door and got in behind the wheel, turning on the ignition. The radio instantly blared out. 'Stupid thing,' he muttered as he switched it off. 'I'll see you around, Tory,' he said harshly, before firmly slamming the door shut.

Tory forced herself to remain standing on the gravel drive as he reversed the car before driving off towards the road, even managing a wave of her hand as he drove away.

She only allowed her shoulders to slump once she knew herself totally alone, putting her hands up to her aching temples as she willed herself not to cry. She had come home hoping to find answers to her future, and while she might have decided what she was going to do concerning her career, her personal life was now in a shambles.

How could it be any other way when she knew herself to be in love with Jonathan...?

CHAPTER NINE

'You seem a little preoccupied this evening, love...?' Her mother smiled at her encouragingly. The two of them were together in the sitting room. Tory's mother was watching the national news; Tory was completely lost in thought. A fact her mother had obviously noticed!

'Preoccupied' was a serious understatement! Tory was twenty-four-years old, world-famous, had more money in the bank than she would ever be able to spend in one lifetime—and she was hopelessly in love with a man who thought her capable of making love with him while involved with Rupert!

What a mess!

'Would you get that, love?' her mother prompted as the telephone began to ring out in the hallway. 'Your dad's still outside.'

As long as it wasn't Jonathan on the other end of the line! Although there was no reason why it should be; their parting had been pretty final earlier.

'Yes?' she answered the call warily.

'Is that you, Tory?' came the unmistakably cheerful voice of Madison Byrne.

Née McGuire.

Aka Jonathan's sister...

'It certainly is.' She forced lightness into her own voice. 'What can I do for you?'

'You can tell me how my big brother is,' Madison came back with her usual forthrightness.

Tory tensed. How was she supposed to answer that? She

certainly couldn't tell Madison that her brother had seemed just fine earlier, when he'd made love to her!

'Why don't you ask him yourself?' she answered evasively.

'I have. He's about as forthcoming as a clam!' Madison added disgustedly. 'So I thought I would give you a call and ask if you've seen anything of him.'

Too much, Tory inwardly admitted with a groan. Literally!

'He came here for lunch on Sunday,' Tory answered non-committally. 'And he's popped in several times since. In fact, he was here this morning.' All of which was true, but it didn't exactly tell the full story of those visits. But then, she had a feeling Jonathan wouldn't appreciate his young sister knowing the intimate details of his life!

'How does he seem to you?' Madison asked guardedly.

'That's pretty difficult to answer,' Tory came back lightly, 'as I have no idea what he seems like normally!'

'Of course you don't,' Madison sighed. 'Well, until a couple of years ago that would have been easy to answer; he was my big, strong, dependable, good-fun brother.'

Until a couple of years ago... Those two years again...!

'Well, he's still big and strong,' she answered ruefully. 'Dependable, I'll take your word for.'

'And good fun?'

Tory sighed. She had seen glimpses of humour in Jonathan the last few days, also an ability to laugh at himself, but she didn't think that was what Madison meant.

'He seems to have something on his mind,' she finally replied evasively.

'Still?' Madison sighed heavily. 'I'd hoped—'

'Madison, are you sure you should be talking to me about Jonathan,' Tory cut in firmly. 'I don't believe the man I've come to know the last few days would appreciate us discussing him in this way!'

Madison laughed softly. 'That pretty much sums Jonny up,' she acknowledged. 'But as he isn't saying too much himself, what choice do I have?'

'I think Jonathan would consider he's old enough to take care of himself.' Tory grimaced.

'In other circumstances he would be,' Madison accepted. 'But as my marriage to Gideon was partly instrumental in causing these changes in Jonny, I obviously feel responsible for much of his heartache.'

Tory frowned. She had already considered it might have been Gideon Byrne's marriage to Madison that had caused Jonathan to begin the soul-searching he was now going through. But it still didn't make any sense to her...

'He hasn't discussed any of this with me, Madison.' Once again she was non-committal in her reply.

'In other words, neither should I?' the other woman commented dryly.

'Probably not,' Tory agreed brightly.

'Okay, point taken,' Madison accepted, as brightly. 'Oh, just one more thing before I ring off...'

Tory tensed. 'Yes?'

'It was a great picture of you in the newspapers the other day at your impromptu concert.'

'Thanks,' Tory responded warily.

'I don't suppose the mystery man who accompanied you on Sunday evening could have been Jonny, could he?'

She should have known this telephone call wasn't being as casually made as Madison had initially claimed it was!

She should also have remembered that Madison, as well as being an extremely beautiful and talented actress, was also a highly intelligent and perceptive woman; her looks alone wouldn't have attracted, and held captive a man of Gideon Byrne's calibre...

'Why don't you ask him?' Tory returned.

'Because I'm asking you,' Madison reasoned.

Tory gave a reluctantly appreciative laugh at the other woman's perception. 'And he probably wouldn't give you an answer,' she easily guessed.

'It *was* him on Sunday,' Madison said with happy certainty. 'You obviously know Jonny far too well for him to have just "popped in several times"!' she explained her certainty.

Tory didn't know him at all, not really; somehow, she had just fallen in love with him!

'I repeat what I said a few minutes ago, Madison; Jonathan wouldn't like the two of us talking about him in this way,' she said dully.

'*Jonathan* isn't going to know,' the other woman came back pointedly. 'The family all call him Jonny,' she explained.

'So I believe,' Tory said.

'But not you...?'

'He doesn't seem like a Jonny to me,' she replied—and then wondered if she hadn't said too much. Madison was going to wonder—if he didn't seem like a Jonny to her, what *did* he seem like? 'Just as I've never thought of you as Maddie either,' she added—because that was what the family called Madison!

'Okay, Tory, I've taken up enough of your time for one day,' Madison replied. 'Jonny obviously isn't fading away from lack of food. Or company,' she tacked on softly.

'Madison!' Tory stopped the other woman as she sensed she was about to ring off.

'Yes?' Madison came back innocently.

Too innocently. Tory knew Madison too well herself to

believe she was in the least satisfied with their conversation. Also, the last thing she wanted Madison to do was telephone Jonathan with the intention of questioning him about his relationship with her; Jonathan would jump to the conclusion *she* must have told his sister something about the two of them.

Which she most certainly would never do! After all, what was there to tell…?

'Yes?' Madison prompted again at her silence.

She sighed. 'Madison, don't jump to a lot of conclusions that simply bear no relation to reality. My mother was the one who invited Jonathan to lunch on Sunday—'

'I doubt she invited him into Douglas with you on Sunday evening,' Madison came back teasingly.

'As I remember it, he was the one to do the inviting—' Tory broke off abruptly, realising—too late!—exactly what trap she had fallen into. 'That wasn't very fair, Madison,' she rebuked.

The other woman chuckled her satisfaction. 'Tell me, has Jonny played for you yet?'

'Played…?' she echoed cagily.

'He *has*,' Madison said excitedly. 'What did you think?'

Tory was suddenly overwhelmed by the possibility of having been set up. Oh, not by Jonathan; his surprise— horror!—at her identity as Victory Canan had definitely been genuine. But Madison had known who she was all the time…

'Think?' she repeated distractedly. 'What was I supposed to think?'

'Of his work,' Madison said impatiently. 'Jonny has been writing songs for years. They're good, don't you think?'

Jonathan wrote songs… Had he written the one she had heard him play on Sunday? If he had, then Madison was right; they were good! Was it his songwriting Jonathan had been referring to when he'd told her he wasn't here on holiday?

'Madison, did you know I would be on the island this week?' Tory prompted slowly.

'I had an idea you might be—you once mentioned that you get back to the island during TT as much as possible,' Madison answered vaguely.

'But did you know I would be here this year?' Tory persisted.

'Thelma might have mentioned it before we left the island a couple of weeks ago,' Madison conceded reluctantly.

Her mother might have mentioned it, be damned! Madison had *known* she was going to be at home this week. Just as Gideon had been the one to suggest Jonathan might find the peace and quiet he required on the island...

'You know, Madison, I always believed you to be a very talented and capable woman—I just never realised *how* capable! Just what were you expecting to happen when Jonathan and I met?' she prompted hardly, her hand tightly gripping the receiver.

'Happen?' Madison parroted innocently.

Tory sighed. 'You know, Madison, I'm starting to feel just a little annoyed at what I suspect may have been a set-up on the part of you and Gideon—how much more angry do you think Jonathan is going to feel if he realises the truth?'

'Are you going to tell him?'

After this morning Tory wasn't sure she and Jonathan would ever speak to each other again. But that really wasn't the point!

'Do you think I should?'

'Not if you have any sense,' Madison came back easily. 'And, as I recall, you have a lot of that. Anyway, what's wrong with a little matchmaking?' she added cajolingly.

'Especially as you sing songs and Jonathan writes them. Gideon and I thought the two of you would get on together.'

'I really don't care—!' Tory broke off, breathing deeply to bring her temper back under control. After all, Madison and Gideon were her parents' nearest neighbours. 'For your information, Madison, you're wasting your time where Jonathan and I are concerned. He has made it clear he does not want me to hear any of his songs. In fact, he's let me know in no uncertain terms that he considers Victory Canan to be nothing but a cheap-looking vamp, who may or may not be able to sing!'

'Jonny said that?' his sister gasped disbelievingly.

'More or less,' she said grimly.

'He sounds as if he's still being completely unbearable.' The grimace could be heard in Madison's voice.

'That's putting it mildly.'

'I really am sorry if Jonny has been at all rude to you or your family during his visit there,' his sister apologised wearily. 'I just thought— Well, never mind what I thought; I was obviously wrong. I think I'll give Jonny a call and suggest he goes home; the island obviously isn't doing him any good at all!'

Tory couldn't actually agree with that sentiment. Compared to what he had been like when he'd got off the plane last Saturday, Jonathan was definitely more relaxed and approachable. But as for Madison and Gideon's efforts to matchmake—! What was it about happily married people that made them think they had the right?

'Do that,' Tory advised abruptly.

'Still friends, Tory?' Madison prompted hesitantly.

'Still friends, Madison,' she agreed with a sigh. 'Just leave me to find my own male friends in future, hmm?'

'As long as it isn't Rupert Montgomery!' the other

woman came back with obvious distaste. 'You can do so much better than him, Tory.'

The Byrnes had been in residence on the island during Rupert's last memorable visit to the island—and he had not made a good impression on the couple, either!

'I suppose by much better you're referring to your brother?' Tory observed. 'Well, don't worry, Rupert is definitely out of the picture. But Jonathan isn't even in it,' she stated firmly as the other woman would have spoken.

'Okay, Tory, I get the message,' Madison said. 'I think I'll give Jonny a call, anyway. Take care.'

She rang off.

Leaving Tory staring frustratedly at the now superfluous telephone handset.

She couldn't believe Gideon and Madison had deliberately tried to get Jonathan and herself together!

But they had meant well, she instantly rebuked herself. Even if the two of them hadn't actually come to like each other, there had always been the hope that Tory might like Jonathan's songs.

As she *did* like the one she had partly been allowed to hear. Well…'allowed' was probably overdoing it a bit; Jonathan had been furious when he realised he had an audience.

In fact, she *more* than liked the little of the song she had heard—the wretched thing haunted her! So much so that she wanted to hear the rest of it. 'Pretty', Rupert had called it this morning, when he'd walked into her studio and heard her playing the little she could recall. But it was so much more than that.

And Jonathan was its composer…

Which was a good enough reason for him to refuse to let her hear the rest of it. If she even dared to ask him, that was…!

'...very sad,' her mother was saying. 'It's such a pity that it has to happen.'

Tory had wandered back into the sitting room, still deep in thought about Jonathan's song, and looked up enquiringly now as she had no idea what her mother was talking about.

'There was another accident on the TT course this morning,' her mother explained as she pressed the remote control button to turn off the television, the local news having just finished. 'A young girl in her twenties was killed on the mountain road.' She shook her head. 'It's bad enough when it's one of the competitors; they obviously know the risks they take by taking part. But when it's one of the visiting fans...! They aren't even giving out the poor girl's name yet, as the family haven't been informed. Her poor parents. It's so dreadful for them. I know how I would feel if something like that happened to you,' her mother declared emotionally.

Sadly, it was a fact of the Isle of Man TT Races that, on average, two riders were killed each year, and usually the same amount of visiting fans. Although it didn't seem to deter any of them from returning year after year. Or maybe they all just assumed it would never happen to them...

That was probably nearer the—

Tory became suddenly still, frowning thoughtfully. This morning. A girl in her early twenties. No name yet given out.

Could Jonathan possibly have thought that girl was *her*?

No, of course he couldn't!

Yes, he could, she instantly contradicted herself, as the idea began to take hold. Jonathan had left her in no doubt when they'd parted last night, after Rupert's unexpected arrival, that she would not be seeing him today. But he had then proceeded to telephone from Ramsey this morning, and, when he'd received no answer to that call, he had driven to the farm on his way back home.

She had believed at the time that he was just being his unpredictable self, but now she wasn't so sure...

The radio had been on in his car this morning, when he'd turned on the ignition prior to leaving; she remembered how impatient he had been as he switched it off. Because that was where he had heard the announcement of the accident...?

Maybe she was just being fanciful. Why should it bother Jonathan even if it had been her that was involved in that fatal accident? After all, she meant nothing to him. Did she...?

'Who was that on the telephone, Tory?' her mother asked curiously.

'Madison. Checking up on her brother. I suggested it would be better if she telephoned him and checked for herself.'

Her mother smiled. 'They aren't very alike, are they?' she murmured.

'What do you mean?' Tory tilted her head curiously. Although she knew the answer to that, really—had discovered for herself that not only did Madison and Jonathan look nothing like brother and sister, but their personalities were completely different, too.

'I'm sure you know exactly what I mean, Tory,' her mother chided gently. 'Hard as he tries to hide it, Jonathan is a very troubled man.'

Tory had forgotten just how astute her mother could be!

Her parents were completely happy with their life on the farm, rarely venturing from the island except for the occasional holiday in England, and it was all too easy for people to assume—people like Rupert, that was!—that their minds were as insular as the island obviously was. But they would be very wrong. Her mother was one of the shrewdest people Tory had ever known—could sum a person up after the briefest of acquaintance.

She was right this time, too; Jonathan *was* a troubled man...

'I doubt he would be here at all if he weren't,' Tory conceded heavily. She came to a sudden decision. So sudden she even surprised herself with it! 'Look, Mum, I—I think I'll go out for a walk.'

'This time of night?' Her mother glanced out at the already darkening evening.

She needed time, and space, to think. And if that time and space took her towards the Byrne house, then so be it. There was some invisible force compelling her to go and see Jonathan...

Be honest, Tory, she told herself sternly; you want to see him.

If only to find out if she was right about his reason for arriving here so unexpectedly this morning... Because if she was, surely that must mean Jonathan felt something towards her, too?

'I shouldn't be long,' she told her mother as she pulled on a jacket to ward off the cool of the evening. 'I'll go out the back way so as to avoid any lingering reporters,' she explained; perhaps a couple of die-hards were still lurking about in the hope that they just might manage to snatch a photograph of her with her mystery man!

It was ironic really—because he was actually only yards away!

She could see the lights on in the Byrne house as she strolled along the edge of the field in that direction, so at least Jonathan was at home.

After this morning, Tory had no idea what her reception would be, but her feet kept walking in that direction anyway. Let's face it, she told herself, even if Jonathan keeps me standing on the doorstep, it certainly won't be the first time he's been rude to me in that way!

It felt as if her heart was in her throat as she rang the doorbell and waited for Jonathan to open the door. What was she going to say to him? What could she say to him? How—?

'Yes?'

Tory's breath held, and stuck in her throat, as Jonathan suddenly stood in the open doorway. He looked even more remotely unapproachable than normal—if that were possible!—dressed all in black—black shirt and black denims—his expression grim as he looked at her with questioning grey eyes.

She moistened dry lips, looking up at him from beneath thick dark lashes. 'I— You said this morning that we needed to talk.'

His mouth twisted mockingly. 'As I recall, you told me there was no need,' he reminded her.

Tory's head went up, her chin jutting forward challengingly. 'I've changed my mind.'

Jonathan gave a mocking inclination of his head as he stepped back to allow her to enter. 'That's a woman's prerogative, I believe,' he drawled derisively.

Her cheeks were flushed as she preceded him into the comfortable sitting room. He must have been sitting in here when she arrived; there was a glass of whisky on the coffee table in front of the sofa, his guitar was lying on the latter, with sheets of music scattered over the cushions.

He must have been playing when she arrived! It was the opening she had been hoping for.

She turned to face him, hands tightly clenched together in front of her. 'The song you were playing on Sunday evening...' she began tentatively.

'What about it?' he demanded harshly, his previous almost lazy mockery banished to be replaced with aggression.

Tory held up her hands defensively. 'I only want to know who wrote it,' she soothed. 'You see—'

'But you know who wrote it, Tory,' he cut in accusingly. 'My sister told you during your conversation on the telephone earlier,' he scorned.

Oh! She had hoped Madison wouldn't already have telephoned him!

She gave a deep sigh. 'Okay, so that wasn't very well done. But it doesn't alter the fact that I want to talk to you about that song. And any others that you might have written.'

'Why?'

'Look, Jonathan,' she said, 'it wasn't particularly easy for me to come over here this evening—'

'Then why did you?' he rasped scathingly.

Her eyes flashed deeply blue. 'I'm beginning to wonder,' she bit out through gritted teeth.

But she wasn't really. She was here because she couldn't stay away, knew herself to be in love with this arrogant, pig-headed, hurting man!

'Do you think I could have one of those?' She nodded in the direction of the glass of whisky on the coffee table.

'Why not?' He moved to the tray of drinks on the side-dresser, pouring an inch of whisky into the bottom of a glass before handing it to her. 'Dutch courage, Tory?' he taunted hardly.

'Manx, actually.' She took a swallow of the whisky, gasping as the fiery liquid burnt the back of her throat. 'I've always hated the stuff.' She grimaced as she put the glass down on the table next to Jonathan's.

'Then why drink it?' He shrugged. 'I'll get you a glass

of red wine, instead.' He had gone from the room before Tory could stop him.

Not that she particularly wanted to, feeling as if, with Jonathan's brief departure, she could breathe properly for the first time since her arrival. This meeting was turning out to be as difficult as she had thought it would be.

Or maybe she hadn't thought. Because if she had, she probably wouldn't be here at all!

She glanced across at those strewn music sheets, longing to have a really good look at them, sure they were the songs Jonathan had written himself that Madison had told her about. But if Jonathan should return while she was looking at them—!

She winced just at the thought of the explosion that was likely to follow.

'Here you are.' Jonathan returned to hand her the promised glass of wine. 'I raided Gideon's supply of Gevrey-Chambertin once again,' he admitted unrepentantly. 'Why don't you sit down?' he invited. 'If you do, so can I,' he explained, as she was about to refuse.

Those manners instilled in him by his mother once again! 'I'm fine as I am, thanks. But please feel free to sit down yourself.' They might be on a similar level then, rather than Jonathan towering over her in this ominous way.

'You were saying…?' he prompted pointedly as he sat down in one of the armchairs to look up at her with narrowed eyes.

She swallowed hard. 'I was saying that I would very much like to see some of the songs Madison told me you've written.' The words came out forcefully—before she could change her mind!

'And I asked why?' he returned with deceptive mildness, a nerve pulsing in his clenched jaw.

Tory shrugged. 'I'm a singer, therefore I sing songs.'

Jonathan's mouth thinned. 'You're a bit more than that, I believe,' he drawled again. 'In the light of my scathing remarks to you these last few days, my sister has taken great delight in giving me a complete dressing-down about your vast musical achievements. Most of which I already knew, I might add.'

Which begged the question; if he had known, why had he been so damned rude to her?

She shook her head. 'I'm sorry if you have the mistaken impression that I complained to Madison about your remarks—'

'I don't have that impression at all, Tory,' he interrupted. 'I know Madison well enough to realise she will have made up her own mind about the situation.'

What situation?

She had come here to try and sort out the muddle that seemed to have developed between the two of them—and instead she was just becoming more confused.

'Again I ask what possible reason could the famous Victory Canan have for wanting to look at my pitiful dabblings in songwriting?' Jonathan looked at her with hard grey eyes.

She shook her head. 'If the little I heard on Sunday is anything to go by, then they aren't pitiful,' she told him huskily. 'And I would like to see them because I—I—'

'You what, Tory?' he snapped harshly, standing up abruptly, all pretence of relaxation gone. His face looked as if it were carved from granite; his body was taut with anger. 'I don't care what Madison might or might not have said to you on the subject, Tory; I don't need any charitable gestures from you or anyone—'

'I'm not being charitable, damn it!' she burst out indignantly, eyes flashing deeply blue as she glared across the room at him.

'I don't believe you!' Jonathan came back just as fiercely.

She drew herself up to her full height of five feet two inches. 'I am not a liar!'·

'You were lying a short time ago when you pretended you had no idea who wrote that song you heard on Sunday,' he reminded her.

She drew in a sharp breath. 'That wasn't a lie. It was an attempt on my part at being tactful—'

'Then you failed in that attempt,' he rasped. 'Miserably!' he added scornfully.

'Obviously,' she replied. 'My God, Jonathan, are you so wrapped up in self-pity that you can't accept or believe it when someone is genuinely interested—?'

'I'm not wrapped up in self-pity at all.' His voice rose angrily.

She gave a disbelieving snort. 'Then you're doing a damned good job of pretending you are—'

'And just what would you know about it?' he challenged, looking down that long, arrogant nose at her.

'I only have to spend a few minutes in your company to know what your problem is,' she returned gratingly.

'Really?' His voice was dangerously soft now. 'And exactly what *is* my problem?'

Tory was shaking—with anger, and something else. She was angry with Jonathan, yes—very angry—but another part of her wanted to just hold him in her arms, keep him that way until all his hurt and frustration disappeared…!

'I just told you,' she said. 'Self-pity. For reasons I obviously don't understand—'

'Obviously,' Jonathan echoed with hard derision.

'Then tell me,' she implored. 'Jonathan, talk to me!' she encouraged.

He didn't actually move, and yet his emotional withdrawal from her was nonetheless tangible for all that. 'So far in our acquaintance talking doesn't seem to have been too successful between the two of us,' he muttered, his narrowed grey gaze holding her immobile as he did finally move, coming to stand dangerously close to Tory now. 'I think I've come to prefer our other means of communication,' he murmured, before his head lowered and his mouth claimed hers.

Not like this, Tory cried inwardly.

Because as Jonathan drew her close into him, the hard outline of his body firmly pressed against hers, his mouth kissing hers with a thoroughness that left her breathless, Tory knew Jonathan didn't intend stopping this time, that he intended making love to her.

Completely.

Thoroughly.

She also knew that, loving him as she did, she didn't have the strength or will-power to stop him...

CHAPTER TEN

SHE couldn't allow this to happen, Tory cried inwardly.

Not like this.

Not without love!

She pushed against his chest, wrenching her mouth free of his. 'No, Jonathan!' she groaned, shaking her head, tears swimming in her eyes as she looked up at him pleadingly.

There was a dark flush on his cheeks, and his eyes appeared almost black as he looked down at her disbelievingly. 'Why not?' he rasped, his arms still like steel bands about her waist. 'You know that we want each other.'

Oh, yes, she knew that, could be in no doubt of her own feelings—just as she was only too aware that Jonathan desired her physically. It was just that she wanted so much more from him than that. And she knew, even more so after the last few minutes' candid conversation, that Jonathan didn't have anything more than physical desire to give her.

'Do you really think I'm going to leave myself open to the accusation that I made love with you merely to get my hands on your songs?' Her mouth curved derisively, though that derision was directed, she knew, mainly towards herself.

Jonathan looked taken aback, his arms dropping back to his sides as he released her. 'I would never—'

'Oh, yes, you would,' Tory said with certainty, stepping back from the seduction of his physical warmth. 'And probably much more besides!' She was under no illusions concerning Jonathan's opinion of her.

He looked at her wordlessly for several long seconds,

grey eyes icy now. 'You have a very low opinion of me,' he finally murmured.

'Not of you, Jonathan.' She shook her head, her accompanying smile completely without humour. 'Just people in general.' Goodness knew she'd had her own fair share of people using her!

'I have never considered myself to be part of the general populace!' he snapped.

Tory shrugged. 'Nevertheless, I don't want there to be any room for misunderstanding. I'm—I have a need of new material, different from my usual style.' She remained cagey on the subject because she hadn't even told Stephen James yet that she intended taking up his offer! 'Something like I heard you playing on Sunday,' she added determinedly.

Jonathan's gaze remained icy. 'Excuse me if I remain sceptical, Tory, but I sense the interference of my sister and Gideon behind all this.'

'Sense all you like,' she answered impatiently. 'I'm no more a charitable organisation than you are a charity case. If I like your songs—and it's still a big if,' she stated firmly, 'then there would be a contract drawn up between us, with everything done in a completely businesslike manner.'

Jonathan still looked sceptical. 'I can already see a problem with that...'

She eyed him warily. 'Yes?'

He gave a mocking inclination of his head. 'They aren't songs, Tory. I write music; there are no words.'

'But that's even better,' she said excitedly. 'I could put my own words to your music—'

'I don't think so,' he cut in hardly.

'Why ever not?' Tory could hardly contain her impatience with his stubbornness. Why did he bother to write music if he never intended anyone to hear it?

'Because I don't write Victory Canan-type songs,' he told her arrogantly.

'I've just told you—!' She broke off, breathing deeply in her agitation. 'I'm interested in doing something different, Jonathan.' She spoke more calmly; having both of them lose their temper wasn't going to get them anywhere!

He shook his head. 'Not with my music,' he bit out scathingly.

Her eyes narrowed angrily in spite of her earlier attempt to hold onto her temper. 'Do you think Victory Canan might contaminate it?'

Jonathan sighed, moving to stand next to the unlit fireplace. 'Believe it or not, Tory, I write love-songs—without words, granted. But, nevertheless, you only have to listen to them to know they're love-songs.'

'And Victory Canan doesn't sing love-songs,' she acknowledged dryly. 'But that's the whole point; I'm going to!' She had read Stephen James's play, and the underlying theme was most definitely of love. 'I'm thinking of—I've been offered the chance to star in a play, the main female role being that of a singer.' There—she had said it, and it hadn't been so bad, after all. She might even get used to the idea herself eventually!

Jonathan shook his head. 'It isn't what your fans expect of you—'

'Do you think I don't know that?' she replied. 'It's the reason I've taken so long to make my decision.' But, having made it, she now intended seeing it through.

'The reason you're on the island?' Jonathan guessed astutely.

'Partly,' she conceded. 'Isn't it the same for you?' she enquired.

He stiffened, grey eyes enigmatic. 'What do you mean?'

'You obviously came here to wrestle with your own demons—'

'Exactly what has Maddie been telling you?' he demanded harshly.

'—whatever they might be,' Tory finished determinedly, meeting his challenging gaze unflinchingly.

'The implication being that Maddie hasn't told you anything,' Jonathan muttered scathingly. 'Forgive me if I find that hard to believe—'

'No, I don't forgive you,' Tory cut in heatedly. 'Madison is your sister; she would no more break your confidence than she would Gideon's!'

'Why bring Gideon into this?' he demanded again, through gritted teeth.

'Look, Jonathan,' she said wearily, 'I have no idea what your problem is with your brother-in-law—'

'My problem is that he isn't only my brother-in-law!' Jonathan rasped.

Tory looked at him searchingly. But she could learn nothing from his expression—his eyes hard, his face an angry mask.

She shook her head. 'I don't understand you.'

'No?' he replied sceptically.

'No,' she echoed impatiently. 'Jonathan, why do you hate Gideon so much?'

'Hate him?' He looked stunned at the statement. 'I don't hate Gideon, Tory.' He shook his head dazedly. 'How could I?' he protested emotionally. 'He's my brother!'

'I realise that by marrying Madison he has become so, but that doesn't mean you have to like him—' Tory broke off as Jonathan once again shook his head. 'No?' she said uncertainly.

'He really is my brother, Tory,' Jonathan ground out. 'Look at us!' He picked up a framed photograph of

Madison and Gideon that stood on the sideboard, holding it up beside his own face. 'Can't you see the likeness?'

Of course she could. Hadn't she already noted to herself Jonathan's resemblance to Gideon rather than Madison? The two men having the same colouring, the same arrogance of expression? But she had thought at the time it was merely an accidental surface likeness...

Was Jonathan now saying that wasn't the case at all?

Jonathan put the photograph back on the sideboard, face down, turning away to stare sightlessly out of the window. Darkness had fallen completely by this time. 'Until I was eighteen, and my mother told me the truth concerning my birth, I believed Malcolm McGuire was my father,' he said softly.

So softly Madison could barely hear him. But she had no intention of interrupting him, sensing that he needed to talk to someone. Even her!

'Even after my mother had told me the truth it made no difference to me,' Jonathan continued huskily. 'Malcolm had always treated me exactly as if I were his son and my mother obviously loved me. Maddie adored all of us, and was adored in return.' An affectionate smile shattered that hard countenance for a moment. 'It wasn't important, you see.' He turned back to Tory, his eyes that dark grey of their first meeting.

She believed she was beginning to see... That conversation they had here the evening they'd had dinner together, concerning Gideon's father, John Byrne... Jonathan wondering if they were all only the genes inherited from their parents... At the time she had thought it was because Jonathan was concerned Gideon might turn into the drunken adulterer his father had been before his death. But if Jonathan really were Gideon's brother, that made John Byrne *his* father, too...!

'But Madison and Gideon falling in love changed that?' she guessed.

Jonathan gave a humourless smile. 'It shouldn't have done.'

'But it did?' Tory persisted.

He nodded. 'From the age of eighteen I was aware that I had a half-brother—the film director Gideon Byrne—but I was happy with my lot in life, and he was completely unaware of my existence, so I considered things were better left as they were.'

'And then Madison met Gideon.' Tory grimaced—not at the chances of Madison and Gideon meeting—Madison was an actress and Gideon was a film director, there had been every chance that they would meet at some stage in their career—but at the fact they should fall in love with each other!

Jonathan gave a shaky sigh. '"And then Madison met Gideon,"' he echoed heavily. 'Sounds like the title of a film, doesn't it? The really stupid thing about all this is that *I* was the one to talk Gideon out of throwing it all away with Madison, once he had learnt the truth of who my mother was—who I was. And I was right about them. They should be together. It just never occurred to me when I was helping their relationship along that I would end up as the one with the unresolved emotional baggage!'

It hadn't occurred to him, but it was easy for Tory—at least—to see that it had always been a possibility. Easy to see too, now, why Jonathan had seemed to be going through some sort of identity crisis when he'd arrived on the island—what she had teasingly referred to as his 'early mid-life crisis'!

Except that none of this situation was in the least funny to this emotionally confused man...

Malcolm McGuire—to his credit—had always been a

loving father to Jonathan, just as Susan Delaney had no doubt loved her son. But none of that changed the fact—for Jonathan, at least—that his real father was a man he had never known, a man he never *could* have known. Because he had been killed in a car crash before Jonathan was even born. And, despite the twelve or thirteen years of un-interest in the subject that had elapsed after Jonathan had been told about his real father, it must nevertheless have brought the situation to a head for Jonathan once he had actually met his half-brother—two years ago...

Because he hadn't just *met* Gideon; he had welcomed him into his own family as his brother-in-law!

'Have you talked to Gideon about his—your—father?' Tory prompted.

'No,' Jonathan replied harshly. 'Why should I?' His eyes glittered resentfully.

'Because you need to?'

He shook his head. 'That's ridiculous—'

'Why is it?' Tory persistcd.

'Because John Byrne has no bearing on my life. The man has been dead for over thirty years—'

'But you didn't even know of his existence as your father until you were eighteen,' Tory reasoned.

'What the hell does that have to do with anything?' Jonathan rasped coldly.

'You don't really need me to tell you that,' she said gently.

His eyes narrowed icily, his mouth a grim slash in a face that looked carved out of granite. 'Since when did you be-come a psychologist? Even an amateur one!' he bit back scathingly.

Tory refused to rise to the insult, knowing that was ex-actly what Jonathan wanted. In fact, he wanted to keep everyone at a safe emotional distance from him at the moment!

'I didn't,' she acknowledged lightly. 'I just know that if I were in the same position—'

'But you aren't,' he scorned. 'You had your safe island childhood, with your safe, loving parents. Now you have your safe, successful career—what can you possibly know of questioning the very fabric of who and what you are?'

Was this the time to tell him of her own adoption? Of the fact that she had never needed to know who her real parents were, what they had been like as people, because the parents who had chosen her as their child had given her all the security and confidence in herself that she could ever need?

She looked searchingly at Jonathan, saw the strain, the pain, the uncertainty—and knew that the parallel of her own adoption was not something he would welcome at this moment! It was his own parentage he was concerned with, no one else's!

'I said *if* I were in the same position,' she pointed out gently.

'Which you aren't!' he responded forcefully.

'Don't you think you're going about all of this from the wrong angle, Jonathan?'

His eyes narrowed to icy slits. 'What does *that* mean?'

She sighed. 'It appears to me— It appears to me,' she repeated as he gave a disparaging snort, 'that it's who you are, what you've done with your own life that's important, not who and what your parents were or are. I very much doubt you've ever expected to succeed on the fact that your mother is Susan Delaney—'

'Certainly not!' he rasped.

Tory nodded. 'Just as you shouldn't expect to fail because your father was John Byrne!'

Jonathan looked at her wordlessly for several long seconds, mouth tight, eyes still glacial. 'Back to the amateur psychology again?' he finally murmured derisively.

'If you like.'

'I don't like,' he rejoined insultingly.

Tory sighed, realising that she wasn't getting through to this man at all. 'Tell me, Jonathan,' she said quietly. 'How do you think Malcolm feels about all this?'

He looked startled. 'Malcolm? I don't think—'

'No, you obviously don't,' she accepted. 'But you said yourself the man has always treated you as his son—something he had obviously known you weren't from the beginning of his marriage to your mother. It seems to have made no difference to his love and pride in you as his own son. As evidenced by the fact that you run his family business,' she pointed out. 'How do you think all this soul-searching on your part, since Madison married Gideon, is affecting him?'

She watched the emotions chasing across Jonathan's normally guarded expression, clearly saw the confusion, the pain, the dismay, as the full import of her words struck home.

Despite encouragement by her adopted parents, Tory had never had any interest in knowing who her real parents were, and she had seen the relief and love on Thelma and Dan's faces when she'd told them that. Obviously Jonathan couldn't meet his real father, but she could well imagine Malcolm McGuire's hurt confusion at Jonathan's behaviour the last couple of years.

'My feelings concerning Gideon as my brother and John Byrne as my father have no bearing on the love and respect I have always felt for Malcolm,' Jonathan finally said stiffly.

'Does he know that?'

'You—'

'After all, you're here, not there,' she continued determinedly, knowing that Jonathan was going to hate her—even more than he already did—for bringing this painful truth home to him. But if Jonathan couldn't love her in the way she loved him, she could at least try to reconcile him with his family. 'And Malcolm is presumably running the casino business himself.'

'Like anyone else, I'm entitled to a holiday,' Jonathan snapped.

She gave an acknowledging inclination of her head. 'Anyone else would have told their family where they were going. If only so that they shouldn't worry,' she went on, as he would have interrupted. 'Okay, so Madison and Gideon know, but you weren't even happy about the fact that Gideon had told his own wife—your sister—that you were staying here in their home.'

'I'm thirty-three, Tory, not three; long past the age where I have to tell anyone where I'm going!' Jonathan exclaimed.

She shook her head. 'I'm twenty-four, but I'm still not selfish enough to consider my parents have no right to worry about me.'

'So I'm selfish as well as inconsiderate?' Jonathan said with sarcasm.

'In a word—yes,' she confirmed.

Jonathan drew himself up to his full height—well over six feet—grey eyes as cold as ice, his expression grim. 'I don't remember asking for your opinion,' he told her scathingly.

Tory took a deep breath. No, he hadn't asked for her opinion, and she would rather it had been anyone else other than herself who had told him these home truths—but, in the circumstances, she couldn't think of anyone else who could have done it. Only Madison and Gideon knew exactly where he was, and they were both just too close to the situation to dare to say these things to Jonathan: one his half-sister, the other his half-brother. It was such a muddle of a situation!

'No, you didn't,' she conceded with a sigh. 'But, as I've already told you, I'm very fond of Madison and Gideon.'

His mouth quirked mockingly. 'Exactly the opposite of how you feel about me!'

She swallowed hard. Jonathan's emotions were far too much in turmoil at the moment for him to really know how he felt about anything; he certainly didn't need the complication of hearing that Tory Buchanan, aka Victory Canan, was in love with him!

'Not at all, Jonathan,' she dismissed lightly. 'I have just tried to put myself in your family's shoes. All of them— including yours.'

'And your conclusion?'

He didn't want to hear her conclusion! It was there in that slightly challenging tone, that arrogant tilt to the squareness of his jaw. No, Jonathan didn't really want to hear her opinion...

'Perhaps you should be grateful for what you have, Jonathan; a loving sister and brother, an adorable niece.' Her voice softened affectionately as she thought of Keilly. 'A mother who obviously loves you very much, and a step-father who, although I have never met him—' nor was she ever likely to, either! '—is a man much to be admired.'

'Of course I admire Malcolm,' Jonathan said huskily.

'Then perhaps you should try looking at how he must feel about what happened two years ago,' Tory encouraged pleadingly. 'I realise it must have been difficult for you when Madison and Gideon were married, but how much more difficult it must have been for Malcolm. He suddenly became a complete outsider within his own family.' She frowned at the thought.

As did Jonathan. He had obviously never looked at the complicated situation from this point of view before.

But she could see that he was now! And, if she knew Jonathan half as well as she thought she did, once he had thought about this deeply enough he would come to the right decision; that of going back to America and making his peace with his family.

'I have to get back now, Jonathan,' she told him decisively. 'They'll wonder where I've got to; I told my mother I was just going out for a short walk.'

His mouth twisted mockingly as he followed her out into the hallway. 'And you don't want them to worry about you!'

'Exactly.' She turned at the front door to give him a rueful smile. 'I sincerely hope you come to the right decision, Jonathan,' she concluded, before turning to leave.

Even if that decision meant he went away from her, back to America. Never to be seen again!

She had slept badly, Tory acknowledged bad-temperedly as she staggered down the stairs the next morning, the smell of freshly brewing coffee drawing her down to the kitchen. Her father was obviously up and about already, despite the fact that it was only six-thirty.

It wasn't too difficult to know the reason she had slept badly: Jonathan!

Once in bed the previous evening she hadn't been able to think of anything but Jonathan, and the tangle his life had suddenly seemed to become two years ago.

She sincerely hoped he had listened to her the evening before, for all of his family's sakes, but she somehow had the feeling that all she had succeeded in doing was alienating him from herself, too!

Her father looked up with a smile as she came into the kitchen. 'You're up early, love...'

'You know I never could resist the smell of your coffee.' She poured herself a mug of the strong brew before sitting down opposite her father at the kitchen table, slightly slumped over the steaming mug.

Her father quirked a questioning brow. 'Is that the only reason?' he prompted softly.

Tory frowned. What did he mean? Did she look that bad? A little pale when she'd looked in her bedroom mirror before coming downstairs, but then, it was only six-thirty in the morning!

She shrugged dismissively. 'What else could it be?'

'Jonathan was here earlier,' her father told her.

Tory looked across at him sharply, her frown deeper than ever. 'Jonathan was...?'

He must have had as much trouble sleeping as she had. She only hoped it was for the right reasons!

Her father nodded, grimacing slightly. 'About a quarter to six. I had just got up to check on that ewe I have in the barn.'

Quarter to six! Tory's stomach gave an apprehensive lurch; what on earth had Jonathan been doing here at that time of the morning? Normally an early riser, even her father wouldn't normally have been awake at that time. Only the fact that he had a sick ewe to check on had caused him to rise earlier this morning than his usual six o'clock.

'Jonathan has gone, Tory,' her father continued gently.

'Gone?' she echoed sharply. 'Gone where?'

'To London. On the seven o'clock plane.'

Tory felt her cheeks pale even more as she stared across at her father disbelievingly.

Jonathan had gone!

Left the island!

Just like that. 'Without even saying goodbye?'

'No, not without saying goodbye,' her father said, making Tory aware of the fact that she must have spoken her protest out loud. 'That was the reason he called in here on his way to the airport. He also brought back your mother's clean pie dish,' he said wryly, standing up. 'And he asked me to give you this.' He picked up a large bulky brown envelope from the worktop near the sink.

Tory stared at the envelope unseeingly. Jonathan really had gone...!

She had hoped, once he'd had time to consider some of the things she had said to him the previous evening, that he would return home to America. But not like this! Not without even saying goodbye!

'Aren't you going to open it, Tory?' her father prompted as she made no effort to take the envelope from him.

She stared at the bulky envelope as if it might bite her. As indeed she almost felt it might! What on earth could Jonathan have left for her in the envelope? It looked a bit too large for a goodbye note!

Her hands shook as she took the envelope from her father, fumbling slightly as she ripped open the seal to tip the contents out onto the kitchen table.

Music sheets! Dozens of them!

'Here.' Her father held out a smaller envelope that had fallen out with the music.

Tory stared dazedly at the white envelope. Jonathan seemed to have left her all his music. What would he have written in the letter?

Goodbye, certainly.

But what else?

CHAPTER ELEVEN

'HAVE my parents arrived yet?' Tory asked Stephen huskily as she looked at his reflection behind her in the dressing room mirror, checking her own appearance one last time before she had to go out on stage.

Anyone less like Victory Canan it would be hard to imagine!

The play began with the aging singer lying on what was obviously going to be her deathbed, her thoughts drifting back to memories of her life and career. At the moment Tory's make-up made her look like a seventy-year-old woman.

Which was one of the reasons she had asked her parents not to come backstage before the play. Only one of them! Her main reason was that she was so nervous at this first venture away from her career as a rock star that she could barely speak her teeth were chattering so much!

What if she fell flat on her face as soon as the curtain rose? Not literally, of course; unless she actually fell out of bed! But what if she froze? What if all these months of rehearsal turned out to be a complete waste of time—her own as well as everyone else's? What if she let Stephen down?

She had come to know the portly fifty-year-old quite well over the last six months, knew him as a loving husband to Dorothy, his wife of the last thirty years, as a wonderful father to his son and daughter, and grandfather to six. But she also knew him as a perfectionist where his work was concerned, a man who wouldn't accept anything less than the best. She hoped he still considered her that at the end of their opening evening!

'Your parents are in their box,' Stephen assured her, moving forward to place his hands firmly on her shoulders. 'And don't worry, Tory; you're going to be wonderful,' he told her.

She turned to smile up at him, grateful for his confidence—and sincerely hoping it wasn't going to be misplaced.

The last six months had been the most gruelling Tory had known in her career so far. For one thing, she hadn't appreciated the work that went into a production of this size. Stephen, although one of the most charming men Tory had ever met, was also one of the most exacting. But as director, as well as author of the play, he had a right to be!

'Has— Is there anyone else in the box with them?' she pressed, unable to meet Stephen's gaze now.

'Not yet.' He gave an understanding squeeze of her shoulders. 'But there's still time; the curtain doesn't go up for another ten minutes.'

She was grateful for his comfort, but they both knew they were probably empty words. Jonathan had left her his music six months ago, on the morning he'd left the island so abruptly, but there had necessarily been communication between their lawyers once Tory had decided on the music she wanted to use; there had been no way she could just take it, as his short note had told her to do. Tory had also sent Jonathan two tickets for this evening's show, but a part of her had always known he wouldn't come.

Although that hadn't stopped her hoping!

The last six months hadn't just been gruelling because of the work involved in the play—in fact, the hours she'd had to spend rehearsing, perfecting, had probably been her saviours during those months; less time to sit and brood over Jonathan, and the heartbreaking love she felt towards him.

Rupert, too, had proved a slight diversion, trying every trick he knew to get her to change her mind about this play, to get her back on the road. But the last six months of staying in one place, of knowing exactly where she would be tomorrow, the day after, a month later, had proved one thing to her; she was tired of travelling, of never being in one place long enough to call it home.

When bullying hadn't worked, Rupert had tried to cajole. But even though she had agreed to have dinner with him one evening, had listened to all he'd had to say, she had been totally immune to the Montgomery charm. And remained so!

Jonathan had never needed to use charm, had just been his arrogant if vulnerable self, and even though she hadn't seen or heard from him personally for six months, she still loved him.

But he hadn't even accepted the invitation of those two complimentary tickets to her opening night!

She hadn't realised how much she'd been depending on his being here tonight until Stephen told her he hadn't arrived, and that sinking feeling in her stomach now owed nothing to first-night nerves.

Why hadn't he come? She had thought—

'Your flowers are nice,' Stephen told her almost questioningly as he looked at the colourful blooms that covered most of the dressing table.

There were flowers as well as cards from well-wishing fans, orange roses from her parents, a bouquet from the ever-hopeful Rupert, a wonderful display from Madison and Gideon, who had written to say they couldn't be here because they were filming in Morocco—but not even a card from Jonathan.

Jonathan again! She had to put him out of her mind if she were to get through this complete sell-out of a first night...!

'Five minutes, Tory,' Stephen told her as he stepped back. 'I had better get out front. Don't worry, you're going to be wonderful. Break a leg, hmm?' he added affectionately.

She gave a choked laugh. Tonight was what she had worked so hard for, and yet without Jonathan... She had thought, really believed, that he would put any antagonism from the past behind him, that he would at least want to hear his own music being performed on stage.

She had been wrong...

But her parents were here, she told herself firmly as she walked on stage behind the still drawn curtains, arranging herself in the hospital bed. She owed so much to her parents. She would do this for them.

All her nerves disappeared as the curtain went up, professionalism taking over as she became Marion. It was an exacting role, with Marion's age ranging from twenty to seventy as the play progressed. But as the minutes, and then hours passed, Tory forgot everything but being Marion.

The emotional ending—Marion at seventy, sick and dying, finally reunited with the man she had loved fifty years earlier but given up in favour of her career—left the audience momentarily stunned. And then the thunderous applause threatened to take the roof off the theatre!

Curtain call after curtain call followed, with Stephen joining the cast on stage, and the audience unwilling to let any of them go.

A huge bouquet of mixed flowers, and another of red roses were presented to Tory before she was finally allowed to leave the stage, her tears of happiness blending with the fragrant blooms as she at last allowed herself to look up into the box that contained her parents.

Pride was too mild a word to describe the expressions on their faces. Her mother was openly crying; her father's beaming smile was threatening to split the sides of his mouth.

Tory waved to them before she finally left the stage. All of the cast were kissing and hugging each other now that their first night was over.

'You did it, Tory!' Stephen swept her up in his arms, swinging her round and round in his jubilation, the flowers becoming crushed between the two of them.

'*We* did it,' she corrected laughingly. 'None of us could have done it without you!'

'We all did it!' Stephen released her. 'We're going to run for months, Tory. Months and months!'

She had done it! Really, really done it! She had never known such exhilarated happiness in her life before. Only one thing could have increased her happiness—

No, she mustn't think about Jonathan now! He hadn't even sent a card or telephoned, let alone arrived here himself. Obviously his time on the Isle of Man was an interlude in his life he would rather forget.

As she must forget it...

Easier said than done, she realised as she at last escaped to her dressing room, not putting on the main lights, just staring at her own reflection in the mirror in the illumination of the single lamp. It seemed like only a matter of minutes had passed since she'd left here to go out on stage, whereas in reality it was over two hours ago. Two hours of nerve-racking bliss!

A small scream left her throat as a shadow moved in the darkness reflected behind her. One hand moved to clasp her throat, her eyes widening apprehensively as she turned to confront the intruder.

'Don't be alarmed, Tory,' drawled an achingly familiar voice. Jonathan stepped out of the shadows. 'I come in peace.'

Tory stared at him as if he were the ghost she had first imagined him to be. Where—? How—?

Jonathan gave a lop-sided smile, grey eyes light and smiling, the black evening suit and snowy white shirt he wore suiting his elegant masculinity.

His gaze moved to the array of flowers on the dressing table, his mouth quirking ruefully as he saw the crushed roses. 'You didn't like my flowers?' He raised one dark brow.

Tory blinked, still totally dazed by his unexpected presence here in her dressing room, then glanced at the crushed roses. She had assumed—but Jonathan had sent the red roses?

'You didn't think I would let your first night pass unrecognised, did you?' he said teasingly.

First, second, third and last, if she were honest with herself! But Jonathan was here, after all...

'You saw the play?' She at last managed to find her voice, although it sounded strangely disorientated even to her.

He nodded. 'I sat in the box with your parents.'

She shook her head, frowning. 'I didn't see you.'

'I should hope not,' Jonathan laughed softly. 'Your attention should all have been on stage!'

It had been. Only at the end had she looked up at her parents, and Jonathan hadn't been in the box with them then.

'I came backstage while you were enjoying your much deserved applause.' He seemed to guess some of her thoughts. 'I wanted to give you my congratulations in private,' he added huskily.

She swallowed hard, still totally unnerved at finding him here waiting for her. 'You should have been on stage with us, taking your own bow,' she murmured gruffly.

He shook his head. 'It's your night, Tory. Totally. Absolutely. Your parents are so proud of you,' he declared emotionally. 'As they have every right to be. Your decision to take the risk of a career change paid off, Tory,' he told her happily. 'You were wonderful!'

She drew in a ragged breath, feeling on the verge of tears again. She still couldn't believe he was here!

'How about you?' she prompted quietly. 'Have things worked out for you?' Her own schedule had been so busy the last six months that she hadn't even spoken to Madison on the telephone, let alone actually seen the other woman. Which meant she had heard no news of Jonathan, either…

'I—'

'Tory, you were wonderful!' her mother cried as her parents burst excitedly into the room, bringing Stephen and several other members of the cast in with them. The noise from outside indicated that the celebrations had already begun!

Tory hugged her mother, and then her father, all the time keeping an eye on Jonathan; if he should just leave now, without any further conversation between them—!

'Stephen!' She grabbed his arm as she saw Jonathan edging towards the door. 'That's the composer of our music over there.' She nodded in Jonathan's direction. 'I think he should stay and join the party, don't you?' she encouraged desperately. Jonathan was actually standing in the doorway now, preparing to leave.

'I certainly do,' Stephen agreed in understanding, before crossing the room to talk with the younger man.

Tory didn't see what happened after that. Her few minutes of what she had thought would be peace and quiet were obviously at an end, and more of the ecstatic cast spilled over into her room, blocking the door from view.

Glasses of champagne were thrust into her parents' hands, as well as her own, and the next half an hour was filled with everyone congratulating everyone else, all of them utterly convinced the show was a hit.

Jonathan seemed to have completely disappeared, but as Stephen was missing too Tory decided to think positively, rather than negatively. Jonathan simply couldn't have come all this way just to disappear again before the two of them had had time to say more than hello! Could he...?

'Time we all got changed, I think,' she decided firmly after that half an hour of jubilation. Her curiosity concerning Jonathan was turning to anxiety as the minutes passed without any further sign of him. 'After all, we have a party to go to!' she encouraged lightly as the rest of the cast slowly moved out of her room.

It wasn't until Tory was alone again in her dressing room that she realised she still had on her make-up for playing seventy-year-old Marion—a terminally ill Marion, at that!

What must Jonathan have thought? she groaned inwardly. He hadn't recognised her on the island as Victory Canan when she'd been dressed as Tory Buchanan, but with this aging make-up on, and her hair coloured grey, she wasn't recognisable as either of them—simply looked like an old woman. No wonder Jonathan had decided to beat a hasty retreat!

She reached out a hand and lightly touched the petals of one of the deep red roses Jonathan had had presented to her on stage—crushed red roses, she corrected sadly. Red roses, she knew, meant love, but she mustn't read too much into that. After all, Jonathan hadn't been able to wait to escape once he had given her his verbal congratulations…

The party was in full swing when she arrived at the club half an hour later with her parents, and the three of them were quickly pulled into a crowd of celebrating people.

'I only hope the critics agree with them,' Tory groaned, as Stephen brought his wife over to introduce her to Tory's mother and father.

'How could they possibly do otherwise?'

She turned sharply at the sound of Jonathan's voice, her heart leaping happily at the sight of his dearly familiar face. He had come to the party after all! 'That's the second time this evening your sudden appearance has almost given me a heart attack!' she teased.

He chuckled. 'Then let's hope it's the last time, too. And you need have no fear of the critics, Tory—you were sensational!'

To Tory it seemed as if they were the only two people in the room; all the surrounding noise and chatter faded into the background, only Jonathan was real to her. After dreaming about him for so long, it was a wonderful feeling!

She gave an inclination of her head. 'Thank you.'

He smiled. 'You're more than welcome,' he assured her warmly.

Tory didn't know what else to say to him. In her daydreams concerning him she had said all manner of things to him, explained so much, told him of her love for him. But, faced with the flesh and blood man, she felt completely tongue-tied. She couldn't say any of those things when she had no idea how he now felt about her!

'Didn't Tory do a wonderful job with your music, Jonathan?' Stephen joined them, putting a brotherly arm about her shoulders as he smiled at her beamingly.

Tory saw the way Jonathan's gaze narrowed as he took in that arm about her shoulders, her heart giving a leap as she realised he was not at all pleased by the familiarity.

'There will be a CD of the music released in the next few weeks, of course,' Stephen told the other man conversationally, completely unconcerned by that narrowed grey gaze. 'I hope you're ready for fame and fortune as a songwriter, Jonathan!'

'I doubt it will come to that,' the younger man drawled. 'After all, it's Tory who is the star here.'

'But you're clearly named in the programme as co-writer of the songs,' Stephen told him.

Tory felt the colour enter her cheeks as she saw Jonathan's eyes on her now. Well, what had he expected? That she would take all the credit for the music herself? Though the brief letter he had included in the parcel of music that morning on the island six months ago, had ordered, 'Keep them, Jonathan', that did not mean she had literally taken him at his word!

'Didn't you read the contract before signing it?' She looked concerned.

'I left my lawyers to deal with the details. I gave you the music, Tory, to do with what you would.' His eyes narrowed again as an idea occurred to him. 'Was it because of the music that you sent me the tickets for tonight's show?'

'I—'

'Excuse me, won't you?' Stephen cut in distractedly. 'There's a couple of reporters over there that I have to talk to.'

The silence left behind by Stephen's departure was even more uncomfortable than before. Earlier, Tory just hadn't known what to say to Jonathan—now she feared she had said too much!

'I thought you understood about the music.' She looked up at him frowningly, glad she no longer looked like an old woman in her stage make-up. Now her hair was loose and darkly shining, her black knee-length sequinned dress clinging lovingly to her slender curves.

'Understood what?' Jonathan rasped.

She shook her head. 'I couldn't just *take* it.'

'But I gave it to you.'

Tory gave a glimmer of a smile. 'To use, yes. I accept that. But I wouldn't take credit for something that I didn't do. And Stephen is right. When the album comes out you're going to be famous.'

'Great!' he muttered, his tone implying the opposite.

'Jonathan—' She broke off, biting her lip. 'How are things at home now?'

'"Things"?' he echoed dryly. 'Say what you really mean, Tory. The real question is—have I stopped feeling sorry for myself?'

She shook her head. 'No, I—'

'The answer to that is a definite yes!' he replied. 'You were one hundred per cent right about how my behaviour was affecting Malcolm. He is my father. He always has been. Despite the fame that you now say is imminent, I'm back in the family business where I belong. I have you to thank for showing me that,' he added warmly.

'Me?' She swallowed hard. 'Why me?' She looked up at him warily.

'Why didn't you tell me that night that you're adopted?' he probed softly.

She couldn't quite meet his gaze now. 'Who told you?'

'I read it somewhere—'

'Where?' she interrupted sharply; her adoption had been made much of at the beginning of her career, when fans had wanted to know everything about her, from what she ate for breakfast to what she wore in bed. But no one mentioned her adoption nowadays...

'Somewhere,' Jonathan repeated firmly. 'I must have sounded like a spoilt child to you that night, going on about what I didn't have and never could have—a personal knowledge of my real father—when all the time you had no idea who your father *or* your mother really were!'

'I never wanted to know. But I realise not everyone is the same.'

'I've made my peace with Malcolm and Gideon. I was a fool ever to have let that strained situation develop in the first place. But I was just so caught up in my own self-absorption; it took someone independent of the situation to tell me that.'

'Me!' She grimaced as she remembered the things she had said to him that night.

'You. Don't look so worried, Tory,' he grinned at her. 'You did me a big favour by talking to me so—'

'Bluntly?' she put in apologetically.

'Truthfully,' he corrected. 'So, your change of career is obviously going to be a success, Tory,' he continued briskly. 'I suppose we can also expect to hear wedding bells in the near future, too?'

'Wedding bells...?' she echoed dazedly.

Jonathan looked around the crowded room. 'I must say I'm surprised Montgomery isn't already here, helping you celebrate. I expect he'll be along later—'

'He hasn't been invited,' Tory said firmly. 'I can't imagine what made you think he would be. Our parting was—acrimonious, to say the least!' She pulled a face at the memory of the slanging match that had ensued on the one occasion she had agreed to meet Rupert after beginning rehearsals for the play.

'Parting?' Jonathan repeated. 'But I thought— I saw a

photograph of the two of you together in the newspapers about four months ago. You were just leaving a restaurant together.'

Minutes before the slanging match had begun!

She remembered those photographs: Rupert and Tory smiling for the cameras, neither of them willing to add fuel to the fire of the rumour that the two of them hadn't parted company on the best of terms. It hadn't occurred to her that Jonathan would have seen those photographs, too—and put a completely different interpretation on them!

'I—'

'Tory, the press would like some photographs,' Stephen came over to tell her a little breathlessly, obviously overwhelmed by the positive reaction to his play. 'You too, Jonathan.' He smiled.

'I think I'll give the photo-call a miss, if you don't mind,' Jonathan drawled.

'But I do mind.' Stephen grasped Tory in one hand and Jonathan in the other, walking them determinedly over to where the press waited for them.

Tory was grateful for her director's doggedness, though barely aware of the photographs being taken, the interview that was given. All her chaotic thoughts centred on Jonathan. Had he really thought she and Rupert were still an item? Could that possibly be why she hadn't heard from him personally during the last six months?

She accepted it was rather a big leap in her thought processes, but now that she had actually seen Jonathan again, realised her love for him was as deep as ever, that hope was all that she had!

'Let's go and grab some champagne,' Jonathan whispered when they were at least free to escape and go and sit down.

Minutes later Tory eyed him curiously over the rim of

her champagne glass. 'You hated all that, didn't you?' she said slowly; his impatience and uncomfortableness during the taking of the photographs and the interview had been more than obvious.

'Was it that obvious?'

'I'm afraid so.'

'Strange, really,' he reflected wistfully. 'Part of the problem I've had the last two years—since Madison married Gideon,' he began to explain, 'with the necessity of coming to terms with John Byrne as my father, Gideon as my brother—was that I suddenly felt a partial outsider. They're all so damned artistically talented—'

'But so are you,' Tory protested. 'Your music is beautiful,' she added with feeling.

'Thank you,' he drawled self-mockingly. 'The irony is, Tory, now that I've actually achieved some sort of artistic recognition, according to you and Stephen, I could as well do without it!'

'Don't just take our word for it,' Tory said in reply. 'When the reviews come out tomorrow the musical score is going to receive as much acclaim as the play itself.'

Jonathan paused before taking a much-needed sip of his own champagne.

'When do you return to America?' Tory asked as lightly as she could manage—his answer meant so much to her! If he was going back home to America in the near future, then she doubted there would be much opportunity for them to meet again. But if he was staying on for a few days— or weeks!—she might, by using the play as a talking point, be able to persuade him to at least have lunch with her. Anything would be better than her totally lacking-Jonathan life of the last six months!

Jonathan's expression was suddenly guarded. 'Not for some time,' he answered abruptly.

'Oh?' God, how difficult it was for her to keep her excitement in check!

'We've recently taken over a casino in England, and I'm in charge of making the changes and refurbishments needed,' Jonathan explained casually. 'Tory, the tickets you sent to America, for me to come to the play this evening, were forwarded on to me here; I've been living in London for the last two months.'

Strange how that bubble of excitement could so easily be burst!

Two months!

Jonathan had been in London for two months, and he hadn't so much as telephoned her...!

She moistened suddenly dry lips. 'I see.'

He looked at her with narrowed grey eyes. 'Do you?'

'I think so,' she sighed.

'Somehow I doubt that.' Jonathan shook his head disbelievingly. 'Tory, I behaved very badly during that week on the Isle of Man. I was arrogant, insulting, judgmental, prejudiced,' he concluded self-disgustedly.

'And?'

He laughed huskily, laughter lines beside his eyes and mouth now. 'Isn't that enough to be going on with?'

She shook her head, her hair moving silkily on her shoulders. 'I didn't mean it that way! Possibly you were all of those things—I'll take your word for it,' she said brightly as he would have spoken. 'But, in the circumstances, those emotions were understandable.'

Jonathan shook his head. 'No, they weren't,' he insisted grimly. 'And it's because they weren't that—' He broke off abruptly, scowling darkly.

'Yes?' Tory was sitting on the edge of her seat now, desperate for him to say something—anything!—that would give her the courage to say the things she wanted to.

'You've obviously been busy with the play the last six months—'

'Even so, I've had some leisure time,' she protested.

'I thought that was spent with Montgomery!'

'And now that you know it wasn't?'

Jonathan exhaled sharply. 'I had no right—'

'You had every right!' she cried emotionally, tense in her seat now. 'Jonathan, I don't believe that you know me so little, that you're so caught up in my Victory Canan persona, that you aren't well aware of the fact that I do not go around making love with men I care nothing about!'

'We didn't make love,' he denied.

'As good as!'

'No, Tory,' he gave a wistful smile. 'Believe me, if the two of us had made love, there would be no "as good as" about it!'

It was that wistfulness that gave her the courage to say her next words. 'I have no idea, Jonathan,' she told him. 'You see—' she raised her head to meet his gaze unflinchingly '—my parents brought me up to believe that love is the most necessary ingredient to any intimate relationship. Which is why the closest I've ever come to making love with any man was that one time with you.'

The jolt her words had given him was clearly visible. He was obviously taken aback, his gaze searching on her now flushed face. 'Tory...?' he finally managed gruffly.

'Jonathan.' She physically couldn't say any more than his name—wondered if she had already said too much.

He swallowed hard. 'I—will you meet me tomorrow? Have lunch with me?'

Her breath caught in her throat, her pulse racing as she gambled everything on the next few words. 'Every day of my life, if you want me to.' Tears swam in her deep blue eyes.

Something like pain flashed across Jonathan's face, his eyes dark with that same pain. 'Tory, what have I done to us these last six months?' he groaned achingly.

Well, at least he hadn't openly rejected her! 'Wasted time?' She looked at him tearfully.

He looked around them, obviously suddenly impatient with the noise and people that surrounded them. 'Are you going to mind if I take you out of here for a while?' he asked throatily. 'I have an urgent need to kiss you until neither of us can stand up!' He put his champagne glass down on the table before reaching out and taking both her hands in his. 'Tory, I believe I have been incredibly stupid the last six months, but I would dearly like to rectify that!'

She gave a choked laugh. 'Rectify away,' she invited emotionally.

He stood up, pulling her close against him. 'Before I do that, I would like to accept your earlier offer.' He gazed down at her intently. 'Marry me, Victory Buchanan!'

Tory gulped, staring up at him disbelievingly. 'Do you mean it?' she finally managed to gasp.

'With every breath in my body!' he assured her vehemently, his arms tightening about her. 'These last six months have been a living hell. A time when I didn't dare even begin to hope that you might return my feelings for you.'

'Feelings…?' she repeated wonderingly.

'I love you, Tory,' he told her fiercely. 'I think I have from the moment I saw you at the airport!'

'You were furious when you realised I was there to meet you at Madison's request!' she protested half-heartedly. Jonathan loved her! It was more than she had ever hoped for…!

'That wasn't the first moment I saw you, Tory.' He rested his forehead on hers, grey eyes gazing into hers. 'I noticed you the moment I came through from baggage reclaim, and I was totally bowled over by the way you looked. That's probably the reason why I didn't see the huge placard you were holding up with my name on it!' he groaned with self-derision.

Tory looked up at him with love-filled eyes. 'No one would ever have guessed,' she said, her heart singing, her pulse racing. Jonathan loved her!

'No, well...' He gave a self-conscious grimace. 'I had come to the island to think—not be totally mesmerised by a black-haired, blue-eyed witch called Tory Buchanan!'

She laughed, her arms about his waist as she rested her head against his chest, instantly aware of his own racing heartbeat. 'That morning you came to the farm, as Rupert was leaving— He isn't important to me, Jonathan. He never has been,' she assured him as she felt the sudden tension in his body. 'We heard on the television later that evening that a girl rider had been killed that morning. Did you—?'

'God, yes...!' Jonathan confirmed raggedly. 'I heard it on the radio. They weren't giving out the woman's name until the family had been informed, and when I telephoned the farm to see if you were there, there was no answer. My imagination went into overdrive! I was terrified it might have been you!' He began to shake at the memory.

'And then when you arrived at the farm it was to find Rupert kissing me,' Tory acknowledged disgustedly. 'That kiss was solely for your benefit, Jonathan. Rupert considered me to be a piece of property that he owned.' She shuddered. 'The photograph you saw of the two of us in the newspaper four months ago was the last occasion on which I saw him—and told him exactly what he could do with the new contract he wanted me to sign with his agency.'

'I'm glad.' Jonathan's arm tightened about her. 'You haven't answered my question yet, Miss Buchanan,' he reminded her.

'Question?' she repeated lightly, wondering if she had ever felt this happy in her life before, and knowing with certainty that she hadn't. 'Well, if I'm going to have lunch with you for the rest of my life, I think it would be nice if we were married to each other first—don't you?' She looked up at him glowingly.

'I can't promise to wait that long—'

'Tory! Jonathan! Come and join the party,' Tory's father invited happily as he strolled over to join them.

'I can wait if you can,' Tory told Jonathan, knowing her parents would be very disappointed if she were to disappear now.

He nodded. 'I've waited all my life for you—I can wait a few hours more!' he murmured, before turning to face her father. 'There's something I need to ask you, Dan...' He turned to wink at Tory before turning his attention back to the older man.

Tory grinned as she stood at his side while he asked her father for her hand in marriage.

Marriage!

She was going to marry the man she loved!

This truly was the happiest night of her life.

So far...

HARLEQUIN® *Presents*

The world's bestselling romance series.

Pick up a Harlequin Presents® novel and you will enter a world of spine-tingling passion and provocative, tantalizing romance!

2002 offers an exciting selection of titles by all your favorite authors.

Are you looking for...?

Cole Cameron's Revenge
#2223, January
by Sandra Marton

The Bellini Bride #2224, January
by Michelle Reid
The Italian's Wife #2235, March
by Lynne Graham

LONDON'S MOST
ELIGIBLE PLAYBOYS

by Sharon Kendrick
The Unlikely Mistress #2227, January
Surrender to the Sheikh
#2233, February
The Mistress's Child #2239, March

Passion™

His Miracle Baby #2232, February
by Kate Walker
A Secret Vengeance #2236, March
by Miranda Lee
The Secret Love Child #2242, April
by Miranda Lee

MISTRESS
TO A
MILLIONAIRE

The Billionaire Affair #2238, March
by Diana Hamilton

**Seduction and
passion guaranteed!**

*Available wherever
Harlequin books are sold.*

HARLEQUIN®
Makes any time special ®

Visit us at www.eHarlequin.com

HPIBCGENP

We're delighted to announce that

is taking place in

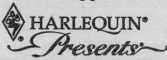

This month, in THE BELLINI BRIDE by Michelle Reid, #2224

Marco Bellini has to choose a suitable wife.
Will he make an honest woman of his
beautiful mistress, Antonia?

**In March you are invited to the wedding of
Rio Lombardi and Holly Samson
in THE ITALIAN'S WIFE by Lynne Graham, #2235**

When Holly, a homeless young woman, collapses in front of
Rio Lombardi's limousine, he feels compelled to take her and
her baby son home with him. Holly can't believe it when Rio
lavishes her with food, clothes…and a wedding ring.…

Harlequin Presents®
The world's bestselling romance series.
Seduction and passion guaranteed!

Available wherever Harlequin books are sold.

Makes any time special ®
Visit us at www.eHarlequin.com

HPJANMM

Coming Next Month

HARLEQUIN *Presents*

THE BEST HAS JUST GOTTEN BETTER!

#2229 THE CITY-GIRL BRIDE Penny Jordan
When elegant city girl Maggie Russell is caught in a country flood, rugged Finn Gordon comes to her rescue. He takes her to his farmhouse, laughs at her impractical designer clothes—and then removes them…piece by piece….

#2230 A RICH MAN'S TOUCH Anne Mather
The arrival of businessman Gabriel Webb in Rachel's life is about to change everything! She isn't prepared when he touches emotions in her that she has carefully hidden away. But is Gabriel interested in only a fleeting affair?

#2231 THE PROSPECTIVE WIFE Kim Lawrence
Matt's family are constantly trying to find him a wife, so he is instantly suspicious of blond, beautiful Kat. She's just as horrified to be suspected of being a prospective wife, but soon the talk of bedding and wedding starts to sound dangerously attractive—to both of them….

#2232 HIS MIRACLE BABY Kate Walker
Morgan didn't know why Ellie had left him. It was obvious she'd still been in love with him. But when he found her, to his shock, she had the most adorable baby girl he'd ever seen. Had Ellie found another man or was this baby Morgan's very own miracle?

#2233 SURRENDER TO THE SHEIKH Sharon Kendrick
The last thing Rose expected was to go on assignment to Prince Khalim's kingdom of Maraban. He treated her more like a princess than an employee. Rose knew she could never really be his princess—but their need for each other was so demanding….

#2234 BY MARRIAGE DIVIDED Lindsay Armstrong
Bryn Wallis chose Fleur as his assistant because marriage was definitely not on her agenda—and that suited him perfectly. The last thing he wanted was any romantic involvement. Only, soon he began to find Fleur irresistible….

HPCNM0102